FLANNEL SHIRTS

Are Ruining My Christmas

SAXON STERLING

DUSKBREAK

Prologue

Isla

So the thing about living in a small town where everybody knows everybody is that everybody knows *everything* about everybody.

Dates of birth. That's a fine example right there. Now, people knowing the ol' D.O.B can come in useful, don't get me wrong. Take dear old Mrs. McCain in the corner shop, and the free bar of chocolate she slides you for your eighth birthday. Fantastic, you know?

But when you're significantly underage and trying to get into a pub for a casual tipple with your girlfriends on Christmas Eve?

Well. It somewhat complicates the process of attempting to gain entrance using a fake ID.

But the geniuses that are myself and my friends will not be so easily beaten, and that's why we've traveled fifteen miles in the back of an extortionate private-hire to the next town over. Here, people still know everybody and they still know everything about everybody, but there's considerably less chance they'll know us.

"What's your star sign?"

That old chestnut.

I feel places on my body sweat which, up until now, I didn't know *could* sweat.

The doorman is big and meaty, with eyes blacker than a coal pit and a head that's reflecting every bit of light from the streetlamps. I sense he can see right through me, but I tilt my chin up, smile a smile that in my head is cool — bordering on cold — and only *just* friendly enough to be confidently polite. "Aries."

I know it's Aries because I memorized it in the taxi over.

When this big, meaty god amongst men nods at me, I think I might possibly faint, but I realize it's just the boulder that's been in my stomach since lunchtime turning into a large pebble. Large, not small, because my sister told me getting in is only half the battle. Getting in doesn't mean *staying in.* But I'll take a pebble over a boulder any day of the week.

We make our way across the sticky green carpet and find a booth a little off the beaten track and a lot out of sight from the bar.

This place is — to put it bluntly — a dive. All dark wood and zero charm. It's called The Doo Cot, the place where pigeons nest and shit, and I don't know why, or who, or how, or *why*, but of all the things you could possibly call a pub you have to question the logic of someone who chooses the place pigeons shit. I reckon it hasn't been decorated since the eighties, and with the red, gold and green foil arrangements taped to every ceiling-tile, I'd say that was the last time they invested in Christmas decorations, too. They do, however, hide the nicotine stains quite nicely and since I'm not supposed to be here, and a pub is a pub, I figure beggars can't be choosers.

"I vote Isla goes to the bar," Jessica tells the group like the red-headed hussy she is. Not a single one of our backsides has hit the seats yet, and *the group* is already nodding in agreement.

Jess has been the ringleader since the first year of high school when she had her minion, Chloe, tap me on the shoulder and invite me to sit with them. Three was enough of a posse for Regina George, but somehow Jess needed six. I figured she was going for a mash-up of The Plastics from *Mean Girls* and The Six Chicks from *Thirteen Going On Thirty*. My fears were confirmed when I got a note handed to me in English stating that tomorrow was jeans and silver jewelry day (with a bright pink highlighter emphasising the *silver*), but she mellowed out a lot after that first term and the six of us have been friends ever since.

"Pretty sure I've done my part," I argue, fishing in my purse for the cigarettes I bought on the way over and holding them up as exhibit A. None of us smoke, but it's what you do, isn't it? When the taxi stopped, I volunteered to buy them — primarily as a test-run of the fake ID, but *also* so I'd be the last one for the bar.

"Exactly," she says, holding up a twenty-pound note and flashing her teeth. "You have a proven track record. And also the biggest boobs."

I laugh at her logic. "And that proves I'm eighteen, how, exactly?"

Jess shrugs. "It doesn't… *but* it gives you a better chance of not getting kicked out if the landlord suspects anything."

I look around the group for some backup and quickly see I've lost this one. After taking their orders, I make my way to the bar, the entire journey thinking about how someone who wasn't here illegally would act. They'd be poised, I'm sure. Casual. Everything would be easy and they wouldn't be acting guilty.

Do I look guilty?

"Three vodka and cokes, and a bottle of rose wine please," I ask the man behind the bar.

"Sure thing, sweetheart."

Sweetheart.

Sweetheart is good.

You don't call someone sweetheart if you suspect they're breaking the law in your business, do you?

Going for casual, I rest my elbow on the bar and look around the pub while the barman pours the drinks. It's busy, and it's still quite early, which means it's bound to get busier. There are the usual older gentlemen sitting on stools beside the bar, eyes glued to the muted horse-racing that's playing on an old TV in the corner. Noise erupts behind them, and I lean forward slightly, but still *very* casually and very poised, to get a better look.

As soon as I spot them, I wonder how we didn't spot them when we walked in.

Not exactly our age — because everyone knows boys never get into pubs underage — but definitely closer to our age than the horse racing enthusiasts beside me. There's at least ten of them, drinking pints and playing darts and laughing. I check each of them over to make sure we don't know them. The last thing we need is someone's big brother blowing our cover. But none of them are recognizable. So far.

There's one more who's just stepped out of the shadows. Tall. Very tall. Brown hair and looking like sin in a pair of dark denim jeans and a navy blue buttoned-up polo-shirt.

The exact moment I'm checking if the face matches the rest of him and confirming it does indeed, he looks up. Right at me. As if he could smell my perverted eyes slithering all over him.

Shit.

I turn away quickly before realizing that just made it look like I was checking him out and got caught in the act. Which, coincidentally, is exactly what happened. But now he definitely knows it.

Feeling my cheeks get hotter and praying the new concealer technique I found on YouTube is working for me, I square the barman up and carry the tray of drinks back to the table.

"We've got bets on which one of those old boys you were staring at," Gemma says. "My money's on the one with the pipe — he's kinda handsome… if you squint enough." She makes the face to match and I can't help laughing at her.

"Don't be daft," I tell them, passing the drinks around. "Hotties over by the pool table."

Every single one of them turns around and looks at the same time.

Subtle.

"Shit," Gemma says. "That's my cousin and his friends."

Cousins are not good because cousins definitely know how old you are. "Cousin? Which one?"

Maybe we can just keep our heads down and remain unnoticed.

"My cousin Lewis. The tall one. Blue polo."

Mr. Handsome as sin is Gemma's cousin?

"Well… let's just try to avoid them," Jess says. "Stay here out of sight and it'll be fine — we just need to avoid the bar as much as possible."

The group agrees, and that's basically an admission that I'll be the one on bar duty for the rest of the night.

But, to my surprise, we somehow manage to pull it off. The drinks are flowing and with each passing hour; the table gets louder and the nerves get lower and the eyesight gets wobblier.

There's a minor heart attack moment when Gemma needs to break the seal and we realize the ladies' bathroom is directly opposite the pool table, but we pull that shit off like a covert military operation and get back to the table, all six of us feeling utterly invincible. Underage? Who?

"Another round, Isla-Doll," Louise says, although more of a slur than a *says*, really. Personally, I think Louise needs a slice of toast more than she needs another drink, but since I'm not her mother, I do as she asks.

I'm bolder now. Much bolder. Me and the barman, Jimmy, have struck up quite the friendship and I'm giggling away to something he's saying while he fetches our drinks.

That's when I feel him. Or sense him. Not sure.

I turn around, because I value personal space and I'm about to tell them exactly this, but my words catch in my throat when I lock eyes with broad, navy blue man-chest. I follow the trail the buttons on his polo have created for me, past the most delicious looking Adam's apple I've ever seen, over the jawline for days, across the slightly too big lips and finally, finally land on a pair of piercing silver eyes.

The strain in my neck has me realizing just how tall he actually is. And the smell! He smells utterly divine, like mischief and danger and temptation and a brand new car all wrapped into one and I *know* that's a terrible analogy but I've had two too many vodkas at this point to care.

"My friend has his eye on your friend," he tells me, leaning down just a fraction of an inch like he expects me to do the rest of the work.

Huh, Well, that's nice and all, but under no circum-stances can we let your friend and my friend get together. That's what I say in my head. Of course not out loud. "Shame we're having a girls' night."

I'm still trying to work out if my tone was icy or flirty long after I've gotten the words out. It needed to be icy, but I really wanted it to be flirty, and I know I shouldn't. Can't. Won't.

The corner of his mouth pulls up in a smile and there's amusement behind his eyes, as if he's taking a good look inside my head and witnessing firsthand the train-wreck that is my inner monologue. "I can do girls' night."

I eye him up and down before glancing at his friends near the pool table. "Sure looks like it."

He catches Jimmy's attention with his hand and orders four pints of lager. "Why don't you come and join us and we'll see who does girls' night better?"

"Not tonight, sweetheart." I smile at him while I pay Jimmy, liking the way *sweetheart* sounds on my tongue. The guy must be at least twenty, and here's me calling him *sweetheart* like I have every right to be here. Like I'm in here calling grown men sweethearts all the damn time.

"You make a shite wing-man," he says. "My friend's gonna be extremely disappointed. Heartbroken, even."

He's close now, closer than he was before. If that's possible. His bare arm is touching mine. And he's warm. Hot. Everything about him is HOT and I need help because if it wasn't for the fact he is my very underage-year-old friend's big cousin, I'd be wing-manning the shit out of this situation.

But it's too risky.

"She's not interested," I tell him with a shrug. A shrug that has my bare arm rubbing right up against his. If this was a movie, or a romance novel, there'd definitely be a big fat jolt of electricity to mark the first time we touch. I know it.

He laughs, and it makes me want to smile too. "What if I said that you were the friend my friend was interested in, and my friend was actually me?"

"I'd tell you that's possibly the worst way I've ever been chatted up. Ever. Congratulations."

His chuckle quickly turns into a smirk, and he rubs the stubble on his chin while he looks down at me. I have the perfect view of his chunky watch, the dark hair on his forearm, the muscles on his… everywhere, and I think I could go to pubs up and down the country for the next twenty years and never be *as* attracted to a man as I am right now to this one.

The fact I'm going to walk away without so much as his number has small pebble levels of weight in my stomach, but I have to. I can't — won't — blow our cover over a boy.

Well… man.

"And I'd tell you that playing hard to get is only going to make me want you more. But I think a girl who looks like you probably knows that. Dance with me?"

"You can't dance to *Feed the World*," I tell him, giggling.

He laughs right back. "That song is one-hundred percent not called that."

I shrug. "Well, they say it enough that it definitely should be."

There's an amused look on his face as he tilts his head to the side. And maybe… something bordering on appreciation? "You're funny. Blunt, but funny."

I swallow. My drinks are on the bar. I could leave — scratch that — I *should* leave, but he's making this difficult. He's not even doing anything. I just don't want to leave his presence. I like his eyes on me.

But staying and engaging more would only lead to one thing — our demise.

"What's your name, darlin'?"

Fuck my life. The way he calls me *darlin'* pretty much guarantees I'm going to hell.

"Isla."

Jimmy puts the last pint on the bar and he hands the money over, telling Jimmy to throw the change in the jar. I eye him up sideways now that his attention is focused elsewhere. He has skin that looks like it would be tanned if it wasn't December in arguably the cloudiest country in the world. It suits his dark brown hair that's kinda messy in a deliberately messy way. All I can think about is reaching up and running my fingers through it. And I'm still thinking about that when he turns his attention back to me, so I take a sip of my drink to distract from the fact he caught me staring. *Again.*

"Queen of the Hebrides."

I chuckle at him. "Never been called that in my life, but I'll take it."

"I'm Lewis," he says, holding his hand out for me to shake. "And you know we'll need to name any babies we have after islands. Wee family tradition."

It takes me a second before the penny drops and I catch his meaning. The Isle of Lewis, Isle of Islay. I almost spit my drink out. He is bold. Capital B. "Barra for a boy and Mull for a girl?"

He grins, revealing a set of straight white teeth my dentist father would be proud of. "You can call them Ulva and Scalpay if you want, you're the queen. Just as long as they're mine…"

I shake my head when he winks at me. "The queen would like to return to her table now."

"One game of pool. You win, I'll let you go. I win, you let me pick you up and take you out on Boxing day."

I eye him up while I take another sip of my drink.

I'm actually pretty good at pool. For three weeks every summer we'd visit my grandparents in Spain, and I'd stay up until midnight playing with my Grandad. I haven't played in a couple of years, but I reckon it's like riding a horse and I've always been the sort of player who aims for one ball and ends up trick-shotting a completely different one. Sometimes several. That is to say, what I lack in skill I make up for with luck.

"Where would you take me?"

He shrugs. "Wherever the fuck you want to go."

"Scalpay."

He grins. His eyes are dancing and it's totally infectious. I know it's risky, wrong, completely forbidden and the worst idea ever… but I want to. Isn't that why people go to pubs in the first place? Drink, have fun, meet your future husband and work out what you're gonna call your kids? Okay, that's definitely the drink talking — but there's something about this guy I can't get enough of.

What's the worst that could happen?

The worst that could happen is he gets us thrown out, but it's almost closing time anyway… "Let me just give the girls their drinks then."

He nods once, sticking his chin out slightly and doing nothing to hide the kind of smile that only happens when you wanted your way and you just found out you got it. "I'll chalk up a wee cue for you, darlin'."

I spend the trip back to the table pondering the logistics of the might-be-mythical Island of Scalpay and picturing things I shouldn't be picturing occurring on a beach that's far more Bahamas than Hebrides… but this is all pure fantasy since I'm absolutely, definitely, going to win.

Right?

Chapter 1

Isla

It was supposed to be a red-eye flight.

I hate when people call them that because I can't decide if it's unnecessarily pretentious or unnecessarily gruesome, but that's what it is. London Gatwick to Edinburgh International, scheduled at five in the morning.

It should have been filled with business folks, just like the hundreds of other *red-eyes* I've done over the last few years.

So why, why, why was I stuck beside a six-year-old who had their iPad on the loudest volume setting, and a group of football fans who spent the entire flight chanting, singing, clapping, and stomping to drown it out?

I clearly underestimated the shift in demographics that occurs over the holiday season. I guess it serves me right for travelling on the Eve of Christmas Eve.

The girls had to twist my arm to get me to agree to this. Since my parents took early retirement and sold up the house and dental practice in Scotland, I've never been back here. I moved to London for work, and since all the family is now in Spain, I've spent every Christmas there for years. December isn't exactly swimming pool weather, but it's not below freezing like it is right now.

That's the only thing I'm thinking about as I cross the busy carpark to the rental place, lashes of icy wet wind pelting the breath — and every last semblance of warmth — right out of me.

I could be in Spain.

Or Paris.

Or Marrakesh.

Or any of the twenty other luxury, and more importantly, warm, locations my company has hotels or spa retreats.

But the girls and I made a drunken promise to each other almost exactly ten years ago to the day. Whatever happened, where ever life took us, we'd all spend a Christmas Eve together in our tiny little town.

It was sort of one of those *there's no place like home* moments that only fifteen-year-olds who make terrible life choices have, but unlike Dorothy, we were intoxicated when we said it.

So. Here I am.

Louise got a good deal on one of those Air B&B's that are ruining every major city and every small town and everything in between the world over. Louise's opinion, and being in the Hotel trade myself I'm secretly inclined to agree with her, but a deal is a deal, you know? Jess and Chloe both live in Glasgow, but Chloe dropped out last minute (sick relative) so Jess is hitching with Louise. Nobody knows what happened to Megan. Joined the army? Working in the UAE as a high-class Escort? Who knows? Maybe she just decided that a promise doesn't count if you're fifteen and can't see straight.

As for Gemma, she never left. Well, she did briefly to study, but then she went back and got married and had a baby and all that good stuff, so she's just popping in on Christmas day.

So The Six Chicks have become The Plastics, and I can't decide if twelve-year-old Jess would be elated or apoplectic, but as I stare down at the car in front of me, I'm wishing three had become two.

"I ordered an SUV?"

The rental guy gives me the nasty eye before shuffling through a big stack of papers, like the internet doesn't exist.

I don't understand because I booked it on the internet.

"Here we are," he says, finally. "Ah. Yes. Unfortunately…"

I already know he's going to tell me they overbook because people don't turn up, and it just so happened that this morning, everyone who got on whatever coloured eye-flight comes before the red one turned up.

Zoning him out, I look down at the car. It's a city car, and probably the smallest one they have available. In fact, I bet you could park the thing sideways and it'd still fit.

Great for cities.

But I'm not going anywhere near a city.

"People have been upgrading left and right. It's this weather, I'll bet."

No shit.

Forecast of heavy snow all weekend, and there's no chance this little lego car could handle dirt roads even *without* a thick layer of snow on top.

He hands me the keys and I just stare at them. "I really need a four-wheel drive."

The man sighs and shrugs, and I'm never a dick to staff because I know what it feels like to be on the receiving end of said dick, but does that still count if the staff forces the dick on you? "I'm afraid I can't help you. This is all we have available. The best I can do is a refund, and that takes seven to ten working days."

He dangles the keys like he's dangling his dickish behaviour.

What else can I do?

After the flight from hell, I don't have the patience to start demanding managers, and I guess once I get there I won't be leaving until the day after Boxing Day anyway. It might not be so bad.

I take the keys with a half-hearted thanks, and the guy is back in his fan-heated tin cabin before I've found the button to unlock it.

Dragging my suitcase to the back of the car, I open up the boot to find it has all the capacity of a stocking.

Back seats it is.

Some amount of wrangling, flicking flickers and pumping up of seats later, I'm off.

The drive is busy. It might be Christmas-Eve-Eve, but it's still rush hour and the traffic on the bypass is foot-on-the-break the entire way. It takes over an hour to get around the city, and the further away I get, the worse the roads become.

There's a steep mountain that has to be crossed, and the only thing I can do is pray the snow gates haven't been closed. The closer I get, the thicker the piles of snow on the sides of the road become. The harder my wipers have to work to clear it from the windscreen. Gates open, the only thing I can do now is push my foot down *hard* on the accelerator and hope the mountain gods are watching over me.

The gap between me and the lucky fucker in the Audi in front widens because there's barely enough power in this thing to get up a speed-bump.

I nearly die of shame when even the massive lorries start to overtake me.

But my tiny little car — who I'm calling Bridget from this moment on — makes it up to the top of the mountain and I'm so delighted with us I don't care.

I don't care that I'm now entering the territory where basic civilized things like roads and streetlamps cease to exist.

I don't care that I had the journey from hell.

I don't care that when I pull up outside the castle, I have absolutely no idea how I'm going to get the damn suitcase out of the back.

And I don't care that the owner of said castle is the blast from my past I never expected to see again.

Except. I *do* care. I definitely, absolutely, care about that.

Chapter 2

Lewis

"Get in here, ya dafty."

She looks at me for a second like she's seriously considering not getting in here, but then she catches herself and follows me inside.

She knows what's good for her.

It's freezing out there, which takes a lot for me to admit since I rarely feel the cold. My old Granny used to say that boy's got a furnace where his parts should be, and, like most women, she was right about most things most of the time. But despite the furnace, I can still feel the chill in the air.

They said it's going to be the worst storm in one-hundred and twenty years.

Unprecidented.

Just like I'm not one for feeling the cold, I'm not one for believing that hyped up shite they spout just to sell newspapers, but my balls can concede there might be some truth in it this time.

I shut the front door behind us and Kimber shakes the snow off her coat, sending flecks of it everywhere — including my eyeball.

"Could you not do that outside, eh?" I'm shaking my head as I trail through to the back kitchen, not giving a solitary tug that my boots are leaving big slushy patches all over the place. I was supposed to have a booking this weekend, so normally I'd try to be at least *slightly* mindful, but I cancelled because of the storm. They — whoever *they* are — put out one of those red weather warnings from midday today, which basically means if you go outside, you die. Or something.

Honestly, I'm glad about it. My cousin-in-law (is that even a thing?), Jamie, suggested I try the whole Air B&B game. I inherited the castle in my grandparent's will five years ago and it's been a thorn between my arse-cheeks ever since.

Don't really have the heart to sell it, but even less of a desire to live in it.

When Jamie suggested renting it, the estate was lying empty and, let me tell you, the upkeep on a massive sixteenth century lump of stone is an absolute bastard. He said it was easy money.

What I should have done is told him to take a run and jump.

What I actually did was believe him.

I shouldn't complain. Whole lot of people would kill for a castle. Whole lotta people *have* killed for a castle over the years. Shouldn't complain, but I will because the money is about as easy as drawing blood from the fucking battlements.

The girls are the worst. Brides. And their sycophants. That's all the rage these days — rent a big place in the middle of nowhere, fill up the car with enough booze to sink a small island, and… well, I don't even know what the fuck they do but I *do* know I'm finding cock-confetti in places nobody should ever have to find cock-confetti long after they've done it.

It was a group of girls this weekend. They said *reunion* on the booking, not bridal party, but I've been stung with that slyness enough times to know that I'd be spending Boxing Day fishing straws — cock straws — out from the back of the sofa.

Not this Boxing Day.

Not my sofa.

Never been so pleased about the worst storm in a century in my life, but it does mean I've had to do the fifteen-mile trip over to make sure the windows are secure and everything's in order before the storm hits.

A few years ago, some tiles blew off, and I was mopping the floors for almost as long as I was hunting cock-confetti.

Never again.

I'm on the second floor when Kimber's ears perk up and her tail starts going like the clappers.

"What is it, dafty? *Hmm?*"

She's whinging at the door, which isn't like her. She only does this at home when company comes knocking, and when I say company, I mean my cousin and her husband, since they're about the only people who ever visit. I'm a collect the mail at the post-office once a week type of man, and she's a *who dat? why dey here? how? I see? I halp? dis new?* type of dog. I'm simple as a spoon and she's thick as a plank. We work.

I climb down off the window-ledge and follow her as she goes bounding down the stairs. There's a car out front — a fucking *Renault Clio*. How that little thing made it through these woods with the amount of snow on the track is a wonder akin to the pyramids as far as I'm concerned, and I have a newfound respect for French car manufacturers.

The respect lasts about as long as it takes me to remember whoever's driving the thing shouldn't be here.

I open the front door and Kimber slides between my legs, doing a circle of eight at full speed. The big wolf loves the snow, so she does. Built for it. I watch her for a minute, appreciating the fact one of us is living our best lives, but shaking my head over how stupid she looks doing it — and that's when my eyes land on the wee lass getting out of the car.

She's unsteady on her feet, the snow almost past her knees. Huffing and panting like Kimber, except Kimber's preparing for *best dey evur* while this girl looks like she's preparing for war.

I watch her for a minute as she wrestles with the seats — it's one of those farcical three-door cars — wondering firstly, why she's bothering and secondly, if I should tell her exactly why she shouldn't be bothering.

I decide to wait.

Why?

Probably my sheer loathing for bridal parties, their cock paraphernalia, and everything they represent.

Let enough of them struggle with their cock-filled suit-cases and maybe, eventually, they'll consider it an unnecessary hassle and stop this madness.

At least that's my logic.

The rustle of a plastic bag alerts Kimber and — thanks to a lifetime of me keeping treats in plastic bags — she's around the car and at the girl's side a moment later.

For as much as I call her a '*dafty*' she really doesn't miss a trick.

Poor dolt thinks she's about to get fed.

It's only with Kimber's arrival the girl notices she's got company. She turns around, and I can practically smell the anxiety from all the way over here. Kimber's a hybrid, but there's just enough wolf in her that someone who's never seen many wolves might think she's the real deal.

The girl is most probably shitting herself.

One whistle and Kimber backs off immediately. The girl lets out a breath that comes out like vapor, clearly pleased that this is a dog, and the dog has an owner, and the owner has it trained to come on command.

She turns around.

Clocks sight of me.

And I almost choke.

Baby blonde hair. Heart-shaped face. The greenest eyes you've ever seen and a witchy look about her to match them.

I know that face.

It's been years.

Jesus, how many years?

I don't even know… but I *do* know that face.

Chapter 3

Isla

ewis Dixon.

Lewis Dixon?

There are a few people I was hoping *not* to bump into when I came back here.

My high school art teacher, for one, because I may or may not have accidentally called him a dick on our last day (he was). The people who purchased our house, for two, because I might have accidentally forgotten to vacuum my bedroom on moving day and believe me when I say it definitely needed it (it did).

And for three: Lewis Dixon.

I can already feel my emotions running away from me.

It's been the day from hell.

The worst flight.

The most horrendous drive in the most ridiculous car.

And now the person I wanted to see least is standing inside the place I'm supposed to be staying for the foreseeable.

I need to chill out. Actually, no — I'm absolutely chilled to the bone — but I definitely need to calm down. It was ten years ago. Almost. Ten years tomorrow. He probably doesn't even remember me.

In fact, I'm convinced he won't remember me.

I repeat that in my head like it's a prayer as I try to lift my suitcase high enough so that it doesn't drag in the snow, and I push away the voice rudely interrupting my prayer by questioning the logic of him not remembering a thing while *I* remember that it's *exactly* ten years tomorrow.

Of course it's logical.

That was probably just one drunken night with one pretty girl in a string of hundreds — maybe thousands — for him.

It was different for me. You always remember your first, don't you? First time in a pub... First time being chatted up... First...

I was a teenager. A horny teenager. Everything feels more *more* when you're a horny teenager.

Right?

"What are you doing here, Isla?"

I glance back up at the front door, only just now realizing that my eyes had been locked on the ground.

He's standing there with his arms crossed over his chest and a frown marring his face.

What's worse is that his face is every bit as handsome as it was when I last saw him.

Even worse, it's actually better. Thirties are treating him well indeed.

And even worse than that? He called me by my name.

He remembers.

"I'm staying here," I tell him. It comes out a bit more stand-offish than I intended it to, but I'm blaming that fully on the weight of this suitcase and the fact it just *will not* drag though the snow nicely making me huffy.

He shakes his head. "No. You're not."

I stop walking.

He raises his chin.

He's *still* holding on to that grudge?

Boy needs to chill out.

And who is he to tell me where I'm staying? What is he even — "What are *you* doing here, Lewis?" I ask it in almost the same tone he asked me (except for the *you* — that required emphasis). But seriously, if Gemma invited him to a girls' weekend without telling us, I'll put sour drops in her Prosecco.

That's against girl code, cousin or no cousin.

"Me? I own the place."

Oh.

So maybe he has a *slightly* bigger right to tell me where I'm staying, or not staying, than I initially considered.

But I still can't shake the feeling he's being a dick about it because it's me.

"Well… we booked it? The rest of the girls are driving down right now, and Gemma is coming over later to see us? Ask her if you don't believe me."

He scratches his head. "Isla…" Sucks in a breath, "I cancelled this morning when they announced the weather warning. It was a Miss Louise Hall who made the booking? Ask *her* if you don't believe me."

When he mimics that last sentence, I seriously wonder if I'd have enough strength to use the suitcase as a bludgeon and would the jail time be worth it.

It would definitely be warmer.

The jail, that is, not the exertion.

Although that'd be warmer too.

With a sigh, I pull my phone out of my back pocket and see that despite having no service right now, there are two missed calls from Louise and one missed call from Jess.

I hit the button to return the call, just in case the signal gods are taking a leaf out of the mountain gods books.

They're not.

The snow is falling thick, so I shove my phone away before the wet gets the better of it.

"I don't…" I don't know what to say. The thought of getting back in that car and even attempting to get on the main road fills me with boulder levels of dread. And Lewis just stands there, staring at me.

The only thing I can do right is lay it on thick. "I don't know what I'm supposed to do? I've been travelling for hours. We don't have anywhere else to go…"

He shakes his head before mumbling something I can't — and don't want to — decipher. Then he looks up at the sky as if asking the big man, or the snow gods, for help, and finally comes over to grab my suitcase.

I follow him inside because if I'm going to be made homeless for Christmas, then I figure it'll be best to let that sink in somewhere warm.

It takes me about five seconds of being inside the castle to realize warmth is not something to be found here.

My teeth rattle.

The trick where you picture yourself soaking in a roasting hot bath tub stopped working the moment I clocked that dog-slash-wolf.

Lewis puts my suitcase down in the middle of the vast entrance hall and turns around to look at me.

I take a quick sweep of the surroundings, mostly to avoid looking at him, and notice more dark wood than you'd find in a small forest and a gorgeous navy blue tartan carpet.

He was wearing a navy blue shirt that night.

The shock of remembering such a small, seemingly insignificant detail has me looking up at him.

Curiosity, mostly.

He's changed.

I mean, of course he has, he's aged ten years.

But I'm not sure that's actually it.

He's lost every bit of boyish softness he once had, but there's more to it than that.

He looks harder now.

Colder.

More intense. Somehow.

I have the urge to ask him how his life has been. Is he married now? Does he have children? Why didn't he leave this place?

But that's all far too forward.

We're practically strangers. Strangers who just happen to know each other's names.

His eyes sweep over me, but I'm too busy staring at him to take much notice until it stops. Abruptly. He turns on his heels and strolls towards the window, stopping with feet planted shoulder-width apart to stare at the thick white drifts outside. "Listen, Isla… If you want to stay here, I won't stop you…" He doesn't turn around. "But I've lived in this place through a storm and I can tell you it's about as much fun as getting shrapnel in your eye."

I fight the urge to laugh at the juxtaposition of what sounds like a joke delivered in the most serious voice I've ever heard. "I'm… I'm sure it'll be fine." It has to be. I literally don't have anywhere else to go. "This building's been here hundreds of years, right? I guess if the worst comes to the worst, we can always walk to Gemma's house."

"Catch yourself on," he says with a scoff. You'd think a person would turn around when they scoff at you, but not him. He stays planted right there. "It's fifteen miles to Gemma's house."

I shrug, despite the fact he can't see it. "I know. I just said that to convince you. The girls will be here tonight, so I can't leave. And even if I could — I don't have anywhere to go."

I really don't. My family is in Spain. It's an eight-hour drive to London where I live, and that's when it's *not*

Christmas, and even if I survived that I'd still need to find a way of getting my Lego-sized car back to Edinburgh Airport.

When he moves his head like he's about to turn around, I wonder if he's going to ask me something. I wonder if maybe he's just as curious about my life as I am about his. But the moment passes quickly when he turns that head movement into a shake. "Whatever. Whatever you want." He shrugs and finally turns around. "Suppose I better give you the tour then."

A strange feeling of something like a memory, a dream, and déjà vu having a baby niggles at me. Did he say something like that before? Whatever I want? Or was it *wherever* I want? There might have been a "*the fuck*" and a cocky grin in there too… But it snaps away when he lets out a piercing whistle, and the dog — or whatever it is — who was outside comes crashing in a few moments later.

"Is it a boy or a girl?"

He looks at me strangely before replying, "She's a bitch."

Technical.

Small talk clearly over, I follow him across the hall and through a set of double wooden doors. "This is the living room. Lounge. Family room. Whatever."

I try to take a peek around, and he's already barging around me to leave. Louise didn't send any photos of the inside, just the initial screenshot of the listing which featured the outside, so I'm curious to see if the interior matches the… *aesthetic*.

If I'm being completely honest, the outside looks like the castle that Jack built. A hodge-podge of turrets and towers and wonky looking windows, with a huge stone balcony jutting out that seems to defy all laws of gravity and physics and which you couldn't pay me a million to stand on.

But the inside? It's actually quite beautiful.

The navy blue tartan carpet continues in here, and while there's still quite a bit of dark wood, it's mostly consigned to a few key pieces of furniture and not the walls like in the hallway.

The paneling in here is a soft white, complementing the powder blue of the upper walls and tying in the more modern looking sofas. There's a midnight chaise on the far side with a bookshelf, a reading lamp, and a side table for tea (and copious amounts of chocolate) and all I can think about is lighting the fire on the back wall and curling up there with a blanket and a book.

Preferably a smutty one.

That's when it occurs to me. I don't know *how* to use a fireplace when it's not lit with LED's and blowing fake heated air at you.

"Lewis?" The sound of his boots, wherever they are in the hall, stops. "Can you show me how it works?"

A moment later, he pops his head around the door.

"The fireplace?"

I nod.

"You never paid for firewood."

"What do you mean we never paid for firewood?"

"I mean there's a ticky box where you can pay thirty pounds for a half-bag of it, and it wasn't ticked."

Jesus. I don't know if I'm jesusing him or Louise, but someone's being jesused. "Okay… so can I pay now? And in the meantime, can we get the heating on?" Before I solidify.

I add the last part as the faintest whisper, but the chuckle that escapes him tells me somehow he heard it. He waves his arm for me to follow him. "The boiler's in the kitchen," he says as he walks through the hall and both me and the dog trail after him — one of us having far more success with keeping up than the other. "Just through here. I keep the wood at my place and honestly, fuck knows if I'll make it back over here tonight, but I'll do my best."

I thank him as we enter the kitchen. The farmhouse style is quite adorable.

And also quite freezing.

There's ice forming *inside* the windows.

He opens a cupboard door and fiddles with something for a good while longer than you'd expect someone who's simply turning the heating on to be fiddling with something.

I rub my hands together, blowing into them occasionally, trying to get the numbness away.

The dog sits watching the cupboard with her tail wagging, and I think it could be one of the cutest things I've ever witnessed, especially if what I read about babies also happens to apply to dogs and I like to believe it does. Did you know that when babies can't see you, they think you've actually gone? Like not just gone out of the room, but completely and utterly **gone**.

I believe the same might be true for dogs because it would explain why they're so over-the-top enthusiastic when you come back.

"What's her name?"

I know… small talk was clearly over, probably still is, but I can't help myself. I've always liked dogs and never been able to have one.

"Kimber," he shouts back.

I call her over and rub her behind the ears.

"Heating's fucked," he says, emerging from the cupboard and wiping his hands on his flannel shirt before running his arm across his brow. He must have removed the coat he was wearing when he was in there, and I've never once wished I had the skills to turn the heating on in a medieval castle before, but since it gets you hot enough to remove your coat, it's now top of my to-learn list.

Except... he didn't turn it on.

What does this mean, exactly? No fire? No heating?

He must read the panic on my face — or catch it in the air — because he holds both his hands up like I'm pointing a rifle directly between his eyes. "Don't fash yourself now. I just need to get a part."

I exhale a breath of sheer relief and nod as if I didn't. "Okay. I guess—"

He's already walking out the door, so I shut my mouth and follow him.

I feel like the bloody dog, chasing his heels.

"The bedrooms are upstairs, can't miss 'em. You get yourself sorted — I'll be back in an hour."

And without a backwards glance he's already out of the front door, Kimber running after him.

Well.

I let out another breath now that I'm alone and can sigh in despair or relief without being judged, and then I close the front door since the thought apparently didn't occur to him.

Of all the ways I thought this day would go, I can safely say this — or anything remotely like this — situation didn't occur to me.

It'll be fine though. That's what I tell myself as I attempt to haul the suitcase up the massive grand staircase. Lewis will fix it — and leave — and the girls will get here, and we'll have the nice, cozy Christmas we planned.

I drag the suitcase up the last section of creaky stairs, feeling slightly warmer already, and try some doors. How many bedrooms did the listing say the place had? I can't remember. They're all mostly the same, each one featuring a big four-poster bed with jewel coloured bedspreads, tapestries, a dresser or wardrobe of some sort, and wood. Lots and lots of dark wood.

The door at the end of the corridor calls to me, probably because I'm a sucker for the black metal decoration on this specific door that sets it apart from the countless plain dark wood ones, and I open it up to find a circular shaped room.

This must be the turret, I guess.

A bed sits in the center, raised up on a platform and covered with silver drapes and a grey fur throw. I cross the room and open the door to reveal an en-suite, complete with a sparking two-person shower and a standalone two-person bath.

Must be the honeymoon suite.

It's stunning.

And it's also mine.

Shame I can't claim the husband that should go with it…

Girl's weekend, Isla.

Right.

I haul my suitcase up onto the bed with visions of cozy flannel pajamas dancing through my head, but my heart sinks when I reach for the lock and find numbers instead of a hole.

It's not my suitcase.

Chapter 4

Lewis

*I*sla Strachan.

Of all the women in the world. Of all the Brides and all their minions. Of all the weekends in the year. Of all the castles in the country.

It had to be that woman, in this bridal party, on this weekend, in my castle, at my door *in the middle of a fucking snow storm.*

What was she thinking? Driving all the way down here in this weather?

Little fool.

Guess she never grew out of her recklessness.

I shift the Discovery Sport into gear and pull away, trying to clear my thoughts and failing miserably.

She's changed a lot since I saw her last.

She's changed, but she's still the most beautiful woman I've ever set eyes on.

Well. I guess that's not technically true, is it? She wasn't the most beautiful woman I'd ever set eyes on back then because she wasn't a fucking woman.

She's certainly a woman now, though.

I brush away that thought just as easily as it came up. No good will come of thinking such thoughts. Notions. That's what my old Granny called thoughts like them.

Notions.

Isla Strachan is a notion.

She's not for me, and she never was.

Best to shove all thoughts about the time I thought she might have been to the place I put the rest of the notions and focus on the things that aren't notions — like fixing that damned boiler.

The car handles the freshly fallen snow like a dream because that's British engineering for you. There's not a chance I'll get that part before Christmas, storm or no storm, so I plan to punt it home, grab the part from *my* boiler, and get it back here before lunchtime. Or, at the very least, Kimber's lunchtime, which is actually dinner, but that's all semantics.

It means I'll have to go without heating and hot water, and I'll have no gas to cook with for a few days, but it's that or a bunch of cold women nipping at my ear and I don't know any man alive who, when faced with such a choice, would consider choosing the gas for more than a split second. That's also a notion if I ever I heard one.

And it's precisely when I'm feeling good about the lack of notions in my plan that I spot it up ahead.

There's a tree where the road should be.

Not a little a dinky tree either, no no. It's a big old bastard of a giant heafin' oak tree.

I stop the car a few meters away and open the door to let Kimber jump out, knowing I should get out too, but not really having the inclination right now.

I need a minute.

Actually, I need a drink.

But I tell myself I'll use that minute later to pour myself a stiff one and jump out of the car, following the trail of paws to where Kim's sniffing around like she's trying to nail whodunnit.

"Shit," I tell her.

She looks up, briefly, and I like to think she's finding it hard to compute exactly why I'm not finding this the most exciting thing that's ever happened, ever.

I walk around it. She pops her head up again, glad to see I'm taking some interest. *Wer goin?* Nowhere, apparently. She follows me. *Whaccha doin?* Honestly, no idea. Couldn't fit a car around here if it was a Renault fucking Clio. She's at my heel now. This is it Da', we're a team Da'. *I halpppp.* Don't need help darling, need a miracle.

And miracles don't happen to people who swear as much as I do. I don't tell her that, though. Well, I've not been telling her any of this, but I suspect everyone who has a dog has telepathy and I keep that part out of it — just in case my suspicions are correct.

I give her a whistle and she follows me back to the car, all excited, like we're off to get reinforcements or something.

That's another notion, though. We're screwed.

Completely screwed.

There is only one road out of here and that road is no more. It's a six-mile walk to the nearest B road, and fifteen miles to the town.

I climb back into the car and get us turned around, unable to picture anything other than Isla and her perfectly raised eyebrow when I break the news to her. For a tiny wee second I'm feeling like the Grinch who stole Christmas, but then I remember it was her own lack of common sense (I won't say stupidity) that brought her here in the first place, and, if she doesn't like it, she's got a long walk ahead of her.

I'm back where I started a few minutes later, standing in the hall. "Isla?"

I wait a second and shout from the bottom of the stairs. "Isla!"

Footsteps.

"Christ, that was quick! You got a death-wish? Driving like that in weather like this?"

I don't. Didn't. But since I'm about to break the news that we're stuck here with no heating, a death-wish isn't sounding like a complete notion…. "There's a tree fallen right over the road. Couldn't get the car out."

She comes into sight, and I almost choke trying to hold back laughter.

"Oh. Right. I'm glad you're finding this situation so utterly hilarious," she shoots, her face all frowny.

And there's that eyebrow.

But it's not the situation — it's her. She's wearing this oversized Rudolph fleecy onesie, complete with hooves to cover her fingers and toes. She has the hood up and everything. And the hood boasts a striking a pair of lopsided antlers.

It's tears I'm holding back now — never mind laughter.

"What the fuck have you got on? What is it? Why does it exist and why… why are you wearing it?" The questions come out in fits because I truly cannot help myself.

She looks down at herself, and her mouth opens in a little *o*. When she looks up, her cheeks are a distinct shade pinker than they were, and the surprised *o* look —

which was honestly bordering on cute, maybe even adorable — is quickly replaced with a look that could kill a cute-bordering-on-adorable thing from a half-mile range. "Are you immune to the temperature in this place? Hmm?"

I do nothing but raise my eyebrows.

"I… there was a problem with my suitcase and this is the warmest thing I have!"

I'm still laughing at her as I walk away, and she's still ranting as she follows me. Apparently, she won't be judged for it, *Lewis*. She's cold, don't I know?

I'm saying nothing.

We might not have firewood, or a working boiler, or gas for the stove, but I've got roughly a thousand tea-light candles stashed around this kitchen and I'm choking on a cup of coffee.

"What are we going to do?" She asks, following me down the hall and into the kitchen.

"We?" I raise a brow, though she doesn't see it. "I'm making coffee. You're… practicing for some sort of nativity. I see no clear *'we'* in this situation darlin'."

She rushes to catch up with me. "That's… not an answer. Can we move the tree?"

I stop the tea-light hunt and stare down at her. "Aye… Aye, let's move the hundred-year-old oak tree. Me on one end, the dog on the other, and you… you taking the middle or guiding the tree with your magical red nose?"

Her hands fly to her hips like there's hip-magnets in those hooves of hers, but I've already resumed the hunt before she can answer. I strike it lucky in the cupboard under the sink and set three up on the worktop, then I grab a cake stand and a wee pot.

"You don't have an electric kettle?"

I roll my eyes. This woman appears to have a knack for making the most ridiculous suggestions disguised as questions. "If I did have an electric kettle, would I be attempting to boil water with a tea-light?"

She snorts and takes a seat at the table. "Guess not. Put enough water in there for two, will you? I'm parched. Also, I think my throat might be slowly freezing over."

I glance back at her, chuckling again and urging myself not to enquire about how much a frozen throat hinders stupid questions. She's resting her chin on her hands and looks deep in thought.

Wonder if it'll freeze before the next one.

"Can we chop the tree up?"

Guess not.

Then again…

Turning around, I rest my hands on the worktop behind me while I think. It's not *the worst* idea.

It'll probably — definitely — take all day, but it's not like we have much else better to do.

"It might work."

"Exactly! Yes. And then we'll have firewood *and* a clear road."

Her face lights up at the suggestion and I can't help smiling. If she thinks I'm going to put live green wood on that fireplace, then she'll find out later just how wrong one woman can be.

"You ever chopped a tree before?" I decide that question is less controversial than *you ever seen a tree before?*

She turns her head towards me. "Me? When I said *we* it was a bit like the last time I said *we* and you said there is no *we*. I thought we'd both assume I meant *you*."

There's a witchy look right there in her eyes as she speaks, like a cross between a dare and a fucking spell, and if you told me right now that I've been transported back to that shitehole Doo' Cot pub and I'm ten years younger, I wouldn't call you a liar.

I've never forgotten that look and I don't really have the words to explain or process what it does to me, so I laugh her off and say the first thing that comes to my head. "You're not in the city anymore, Queen Rudolph."

Chapter 5

Lewis

To give Isla credit where it's due, she carried her own axe for about half a mile before I took pity on her.

Could I have taken the car?

Yes. Absolutely.

So why didn't I?

Same reason I didn't take the chainsaw.

Sheer amusement.

She's now wearing my shirt over the Rudolph suit and an old waxed Barber jacket we found in one of the cupboards. I think my gran bought it when she went through one of her country-Balmoral Queen inspired phases. The fake antlers are blowing all over the place in the wind and I have to keep my eyes trained on Kimber because if I look too long, I start laughing. Again.

"I'm just thinking… why didn't we take the car?"

I fight to keep the smile down. Is it fucked up that there's a big part of me which enjoys teasing her? "Saving fuel in case we need it."

When she nods innocently, I realize the fucked up part is probably the fact I can lie to her and she believes it.

"I didn't realize how far away it was," she mutters.

"Not much further now." Another lie. We're probably only halfway there.

I'm about to start overthinking the hell out of white lies and actual lies and the moral implications of each when I stop myself. She knows all about lies, and I doubt she spent any time at all thinking about implications.

Or consequences.

I glance over my shoulder at her, a few steps behind and trudging her feet and doing her best to angle her small frame against the biting wind which only seems to be getting worse. I left my phone in the car because it doesn't get a signal out here, so I'm not sure what time it is and there's no sun in the sky to clue us in, just thick white fog. I'm guessing, just by the light and how quickly it feels like it's dying, that the weather warning has kicked in already.

Which means technically we shouldn't be out here at all.

But if we don't get this tree out of the way, we'll be stuck here for the foreseeable, and while I could cope with that if it was me and my dog… being stuck here with Isla…?

I'd rather sit on a mousetrap.

Or chop up a tree with a rusty axe in the middle of a blizzard.

Nah, really, I plan to go back, grab the chainsaw and do it myself. Just as soon as she breaks.

It's the least she deserves.

Twenty minutes later, she pipes up again, although the wind doesn't leave much left of her voice. "I thought you said not much further?"

"It's not — just down there," I tell her, nodding my head at the bend in the road since I can't point with hands full of axes.

But the more I look, the more I see the tree is almost completely hidden now, the tire tracks from earlier long gone. If it wasn't for the bend in the road, I wouldn't have known there was supposed to be a tree there.

"I… I can't see any trees?"

I look back to find her stopped in her tracks, blue eyes piercing me harder than the wind and the snow combined, and I always thought there was an inch thick wall of steel surrounding that furnace but apparently it's down for maintenance, or it doesn't work on blue eyes, or she's worked her magic around it because I feel them and it… hurts. "You're actually accusing me of lying? That's a bit rich coming from you, is it not?"

She moves a fraction of an inch back, like I've just fucked around with her ice-box, but she recovers much quicker than I was able to and shoulders me as she passes.

I fight the urge to push her back because she'd probably topple over.

And because we're not twelve.

"That was a long time ago," she argues.

I wait until I've fallen into step beside her before I shrug.

She continues, glancing up like she's checking I'm listening. "And I think you're forgetting — *you* came on to me…"

I came on to her? She was in a pub!

"I mean… it's not like I set out to reel you in or something."

"Never said you did," I tell her. "I'm just saying, you could have come clean at any point."

She looks up at me and this time she keeps looking, her face covered in flecks of snow and her cheeks rosy. "Like I said… it was a long time ago."

Aye, it was. No point crying over spilled milk. That's another notion.

I turn away and neither of us speaks until we get to the place where the tree should be. The only part that's visible now is the top.

Snow is burying everything else.

"We'll need to dig it out before we can chop it up?" she asks.

I let the axes drop to the ground while I go over and investigate. Even with the chainsaw, it's a shitload of work for one person.

When I turn back towards her, I see she's got her arms crossed around her body, shifting from foot to foot. She looks frozen solid.

"Nah." I shake my head and look up at the sky. "This isn't happening. Not today at least."

The weather's getting worse and I could spend the rest of the daylight digging it out, only to find it buried again in the morning.

"I can't stay in that place with no heating," she says. "I'll die. We'll catch hypothermia."

I pick up the axes and start walking back to the castle.

She's being dramatic, and the fact she follows me proves it.

"Humans have been surviving worse storms long before castles were a thing, Isla. Wee bit perspective'll do you good."

Chapter 6

Isla

A wee bit perspective. Isla.

Like it's *that* easy.

I am so, so cold.

My hands are numb. My feet are numb. My nose has gone well beyond numb to the point it's painful.

By the time we get back to the castle, I feel like I'll never be warm again. I feel like I don't know what warmth feels like.

What even is warmth?

Lewis is gone doing who-knows-what, and I came upstairs to dry and attempt to foster some kind of warmth, but without a suitcase I'm totally screwed.

The only reason I have the onesie is because it wouldn't fit in the suitcase, so I had to carry it on, and now it's soaking wet and ice cold.

I peel it off me with fingers that won't do what I need them to do and hit the en-suite in search of towels, surprised to find Lewis had the foresight to realize couples on their honeymoon might go through more than average.

I wrap one around my dripping wet hair, another one around my middle like a maxi-skirt, one for a bodice, then another as a shawl, and I throw one over the top of the hair towel for good measure, letting it drape down the sides and feeling thoroughly like some sort of renaissance queen when I check my reflection in the mirror.

I kinda like it, but my stomach growls in protest when I suck my belly in for the side-angle view.

The girls were supposed to arrive here by lunchtime with the food and drink. Gemma was bringing the food, Jess and Louise the drink, and I picked up a couple of tins of shortbread at the airport to at least acknowledge the fact the car travelers were getting a raw deal.

So now we're stranded with no heating, no proper food, and no way of cooking proper food even if we had some.

Feeling like the day probably can't get any worse, I crawl under the thick bed covers and wrap them tightly around me, my whole body jolting from how cold they are but telling myself it'll be worth it when they heat up.

I'll just give myself ten minutes.

Just until I'm warm.

I wake up and it's dark.

Really dark.

It's not the city dark I'm used to, where it's never actually fully dark because there are always car lights and a constant orange glow from the thousands of streetlamps.

No.

This is one-hundred percent pitch *can't see your hand in front of your face* dark.

But, although I'm still cold, I'm not uncontrollably shaking anymore. Silver linings and all that.

The sound of windows being hammered by the wind is so deafeningly loud, I wonder how I managed to sleep so long, but it felt like the kind of sleep where you wake up not knowing if it's today or a week on Tuesday.

Are the girls here yet?

I pull back the covers and slip out of bed, edging my way along an unfamiliar circular wall and cracking my thigh against an unfamiliar side table. When I finally reach the door, I feel around for a light switch, and after some moments finally locate the little bastard.

I flick it, and nothing happens.

Of course it doesn't.

The castle gods are punishing me for offending the suitcase gods.

The hallway is also in complete darkness, and I don't think I'm familiar enough with the layout to *not* come crashing headfirst down the stairs.

"Lewis?"

When nothing happens, I try again.

No response.

My heart picks up. Slightly. Okay, slightly more than slightly. Funny how darkness and a few loud bangs can cause a complete one-eighty flip on your *People I Never Want To See Again* list, you know?

Blindly, I make my way along the hall, careful not to walk into stuff and hurt my already sore thigh again. When I touch the carved edge of the handrail, I drop my toe down like I'm testing a hot bath.

Bingo.

I take them like any sensible human who doesn't know how to use stairs takes stairs, by sitting down on my backside and bumping.

At the bottom, I call out for Lewis again, and when I get nothing back, I seriously consider the possibility that he might have left me.

I mean… maybe he lives close by and walked home?

It's not beyond the realms of possibility, but it is definitely beyond the realms of being an arsehole.

I sit on my step like I'm six again, and just like any six-year-old sent to the thinking / naughty / I've been a little shit step, my mind wanders and before long I'm picturing him sitting in his nice warm house with his heating cranked up to incineration levels and maybe a nice wood burner in the corner roasting away the oak tree that he secretly chopped up while I was sleeping. Maybe he's got a big fat dinner on his lap. Maybe that dinner is Chinese food and maybe it's piping hot. Yes. The big bastard is so hot in his roasting cozy house he's had to take his shirt off…

I shake myself out of it and give him some pajamas. Really, properly ugly ones. With antlers.

Then I laugh because he looks every bit as ridiculous as I did, and it's what he deserves.

I'm sure the living room was roughly that way, so that's where I go, and I push the door open a creak to reveal… light.

And not just any light. Fire.

We have fire.

I'm so delighted that I take a second to realize Lewis is already sitting in front of it. No layers for him, no towel clothing for this man — of no — he doesn't need to be walking around like a Sister Act extra trying to keep a hold of his tits because he's been toasting himself all afternoon, apparently.

"You put the fire on and didn't tell me?"

He glances over his shoulder and smirks, the dancing firelight making something that was probably supposed to be playful look oddly sinister. "I see sleeping beauty has awoken."

I cross the room and sit down on the carpet beside him, a couple of meters away from the fire and a couple of meters away from him. Instantly, my face warms, and I never thought I could be this happy over a hot face.

"Did you go and chop down a tree, then?"

He wipes his brow with his bare arm, and it's impossible not to notice the way his muscles move when he does it. "Aye, five-foot wide so it was. Took me six hours. Then two to get back, what without your wee red nose to guide me."

Okay, so now I'm feeling a little bad for sleeping all day while he was out playing mountain man. "You didn't happen to catch any… um… *meat* while you were out there, did you?"

He chuckles. "Isla, I never chopped any trees. You need dead trees for firewood. I just broke up some crates from the basement."

I turn around and look at him. His sarcastic attitude is getting right on my towel-tits. "When did you turn into such a condescending arsehole?"

"Oh, I dunno — when did you turn into such a fucking airhead city-dweller?"

"City-dweller!" I snort at him. "It offends you I don't have in-depth, tree-surgeon levels of knowledge about what makes for optimum firewood? Newsflash Lewis: they invented electric fires years ago."

He smirks at me again and then looks back at the fire before replying. "No, Isla. That doesn't offend me — not in the slightest. But it offends me you'd come to stay this far away from civilization, in the middle of winter, in the middle of a shitting snowstorm, with nothing but a shite car for driving, a reindeer suit for wearing, and a tin of fucking shortbread for sustenance."

I shake my head at him. Unbelievable. "And what did you bring, hmm? What's your contribution, oh high-and-mighty one? Some tea-light candles, a useless rusty axe and jar of 1996 instant coffee? My hero!"

"I was here to shutter the windows," he snaps. "I wasn't planning on staying."

"Well, I wasn't planning on losing my suitcase and getting stranded here alone, so that makes two of us. I thought the girls were going to bring food..."

"I thought you were eighteen," he mutters. "Shows what use *thought* is."

I let out a sigh. "Why don't we phone Gemma? We could meet her at the tree, she can drive us to her house? She'll have food?"

"Aye, excellent idea. Except the power's off."

I look up at the ceiling, wondering if it's possible for forces to fuck us — specifically *me* — in any more ways.

Neither of us say anything else.

We both just sit there. Watching the fire. Slowly going demented.

It's a bit like waiting for a bus when you know the service finished four hours ago.

"Why don't we make some of your shite coffee and eat some of my sickeningly overpriced shortbread?"

He looks over at me, and it takes me a full second to read if the smile is a smile or a smirk. I think it's a smile, though, albeit an uneasy one. "Thought you'd never offer."

Chapter 7

Lewis

$\mathcal{I}$ can't really bide black coffee, but it's better than drinking ice cold water, and the sugar on the shortbread helps it go down easier.

"This has nothing on the stuff my gran used to make," I tell her.

We're back in the living room — the only place in the castle that's even vaguely warm. She had come through to the kitchen with me, but after five minutes of waiting on the water to get hot — and listening to her teeth chatter — I sent her to the fire.

Not in a witch trial way, although tempting. More that I took pity on her. Especially considering she's dressed one-hundred percent in towels.

"Is the gran you're talking about the same as Gemma's Gran?"

I nod, and she smiles. "Then I'd have to agree with you. Her mum always kept a tin of it in the kitchen and every Saturday night we'd get fired into it watching Britain's Got Talent with a cup of tea."

I chuckle. As silly as it sounds, I'd forgotten she was Gemma's friend.

"Does she still make it?"

I look down, wondering if she realizes we're sitting in her old living room. "Nah. She passed away five years ago, couple weeks after my granda' died. She left me this place."

"Oh. Sorry to hear that."

"Don't be." I shake my head, taking another drink of coffee and washing it down with shortbread. Fully aware that's arse-over-elbow, but the coffee really is disgusting. "It happens."

"What about your parents?"

I glance over at her. "What about them?"

"You said you inherited this place... where are your parents?"

Jesus. I guess this is what folk did before there was television and Wi-Fi. Talked to eachother. Made an army of children. Tried not to die of the cold. And the syphilis. "It was just me and my grandparents since I was a boy.

They died before I started school. And you don't need to say you're sorry again."

She smiles. "Noted. So… what about you? Are you married? Children?"

I take another drink, wishing it was whisky because this is starting to feel like an inquisition. I know, I know. That's partly my fault. I'm supposed to be asking her questions too — it's called a conversation. Is she married? Where did she go? What does she do when she's not sitting in a frozen castle with the likes of me?

But honestly, I don't want to know.

I don't want to hear about her perfect life in the big city, and how leaving here was the best thing she ever did.

Not interested.

"Never married. No kids."

"Why not?"

I shrug. "Dunno. Maybe I like dogs more than I like people."

She chuckles. "The Lewis I knew didn't come across that way."

I give her a sideways look. "As you said, that was a long time ago."

"Hmm. Well. I didn't get married either," she says before sipping her drink. "I work in a job where it's hard to meet people. I mean, one day I'll come to work and there'll be some crisis in Paris and I'll be on the next flight. We've just opened a new location in Marrakesh and next year we have plans to expand into the Emirates, so it's only going to get worse. Not like you can raise a family when you don't know which continent you'll be on tomorrow, you know?"

I said I didn't want to know, but I get the feeling she'd be telling me all this even if I told her that. Plus… maybe curiosity is getting the better of me. "What is it you do?"

I'm trying to sound like I'm not interested, and, like I suspected, it doesn't seem to phase her in the slightest.

"Oh, I'm a Quality Manager. So we have our flagship hotel in London, and then we have sister hotels in Paris, Rome, and Madrid which I'm responsible for too. Well, jointly responsible. There's two of us, but Charlie's more of a 'things' girl than a people girl, and I think she's going to leave soon. This break was sort of… the last hurrah before things get really crazy next year."

Just like I suspected. She's a city-girl now, through and through. Career woman. And probably a high-class one at that, used to jetting off to all these glamourous places.

It's probably a good thing that night ended the way it did.

We'd never have worked out.

"Sounds interesting."

"It probably sounds better than it is, to be honest. It gets lonely."

I don't comment on that because I can't relate. At all. Sitting in my empty house after a hard day's graft with the dog at my feet, well, I've only ever thought that was bliss.

Lonely isn't a word I identify with.

"So what do you do?" she asks.

"This and that."

"We're stuck together for who knows how long," she says, raising her eyebrow. "It'll go quicker if you work out a way to converse using more than three words."

"I sell firewood."

"That was a three word answer," she bites back.

"So it was."

She's about to clamp me again, but I grin at her, and she giggles. "You're doing that on purpose now."

"No 'um not."

When she turns to me and smiles, I look at her. Really properly look at her. The flames from the fire are casting warm light across her face, making her eyes look like they're dancing.

Or casting spells again.

I swallow because I fucking *know* I should look away. I should, but I can't.

And she's not looking away either.

What's she looking at?

As if she can hear my thoughts, she lowers her long dark lashes and lets out a soundless laugh before looking back into the flames.

"So what do we do now?" she asks, finishing off the last gulp of her coffee.

Good question.

I don't even know what time it is, but judging by how long it's been dark, I'm guessing it's quite late.

The power went out hours ago — probably a fallen line somewhere. It happens from time to time, sometimes it's only an hour or two and sometimes it's days. Either way, tomorrow is going to be long, hard, and tricky.

"I dunno about you, sleeping beauty, but I'm shattered," I admit. I've always been the early to bed type. I like to be up before the crack of dawn and getting on with the day. Never cared much for late nights, not since I was younger.

"I could sleep," she says, shrugging.

"Well, we should both sleep in here. It'll be warm for a while after the fire dies."

She gives me a sideways glance, and I let out a single laugh. "Isla, I think you should know by now that if I wanted in about between your legs, it'd be much more obvious than *that*."

She laughs and shakes her head, rolling her eyes slightly. "Yeah, I guess you were quite… forward."

I shrug, getting up. "Nothing wrong with that. I'm a man who knows what he wants and gets it."

"I'm the same," she bites back.

I look down at her. "What do you want right now?"

"The big sofa."

I laugh. "Alright. Anything for the queen, eh? I'll take the wee one."

"A true gentleman," she says, holding out her hand so I can help her up off the floor.

A gentleman indeed.

Chapter 8

Isla

The howl of the wind is so loud I wake up in a panic.

I've forgotten where I am, who I am, what is life.

The only thing I know for sure is I'm cold.

Seriously cold… again.

I lie still for a few moments, wrapping the covers around me and trying to think warm thoughts.

The storm outside sounds like it's about to come through the windows at any given moment, and this might just be my own treacherous imagination, but it's increasingly impossible to think warm thoughts when visions of *that exact scenario* just will not fucking leave.

I open my eyes and it's the strangest feeling. I can't see anything at all, and since I'm unfamiliar with the room, I can barely even visualize where anything is. The windows, the furniture, Lewis.

All I'm getting is the roaring of the wind, and I don't like it a single bit.

I wonder if he's sleeping?

If he is, I can't wake him up and ask him to put the fire back on, can I?

I really want to, though. It's been years since I've had to deal with all this shit. The wind screaming, whistling, battering everything that's not underground. The power cuts. The bitter cold that's so cold it almost feels wet.

When I was little, I'd sneak into my mum and dad's bed and everything would always seem better in the morning when the world was calm again. Mum would light candles and warm some milk, and Dad would put everything to rights, and life would go on.

I'm not saying I want to sneak into Lewis's bed — which would be impossible since he doesn't have a bed — but the fire, some heat and a little light, that would help.

Could I ask him?

I don't think I'm his favourite person in the world and waking him up would probably just agitate him more than he already seems to be.

But on the other hand, we did make some progress tonight. Well, we actually talked, so I don't feel like we're strangers anymore.

Are we friends?

If we're friends, then it would be totally acceptable to wake him up, wouldn't it?

"Lewis?" The sound which comes out of my mouth is only just loud enough to be heard over the storm. I figure I'll give it three tries, and if he doesn't wake up, then I'll—

"What?" he clips, sounding hoarse and fed up. And definitely, definitely awake.

"Are you awake?"

I know. But it's what you ask, isn't it?

"Aye," he says.

"I'm freezing."

"Aye… me too."

I don't say anything else, now feeling like it would be too much to ask him to go down to the basement for more firewood and wondering why I ever thought it wasn't.

A few moments pass and neither of us say anything and it's awkward.

Like we both know the other one is awake and thinking about what to say next.

Or maybe that's just me imagining it that way. Maybe he's just trying to get back to sleep.

I shiver, wishing he didn't hate me and we didn't have a past and I didn't have to sleep on this sofa alone.

Fuck it.

"Do you want to…"

Nope. Can't do it.

"What?"

"Nothing."

He sighs. "Do I want to what?"

"It doesn't matter."

"Then say it safely with the knowledge that we're both aware it doesn't matter."

Now I'm the one sighing. "I was going to ask if you wanted to share a sofa but like I said, it doesn't matter."

I try to say it confidently, like I'm not dying of internal cringe when I really am. I suddenly feel hotter than I have since I got off the plane.

He says nothing. Of course.

He. Says. Nothing.

At least we've discovered I still have the ability to sweat.

I close my eyes — not that it makes any difference — and let the visions of the wind coming through the windows take over since it's a damn sight better than reliving the last minute of my life.

Then I hear something, barely even audible over the storm, but something nonetheless.

Is he coming over?

No.

Footsteps, but within a few moments, I hear the door opening and closing.

Fabulous.

I've scared him away.

Literally the only human in a twenty(?) mile radius — the only human who knows how to light fires and heat water and fix boilers and chop trees — and I've scared him away.

What a bloody fool.

Or maybe he's the bloody fool. I mean, he could have just said, *nah, I'm fine here thanks Isla.* Now it's going to be completely awkward. As if it wasn't awkward enough already.

But then the door opens again, and he's back. I feel some added weight on top of me and realize it's an extra duvet cover about half a second before I heart-attack the hell out of there.

Relief settles over me like the cover does. I didn't weird him out or piss him off or force him out of the room.

He was just getting me another cover.

And then another.

He puts a third one on top and I feel like a little child being tucked into bed.

"Scootch that little arse over, then," he says expectantly.

I kind of half sit up — which is a struggle with the amount of weight above me — when I feel him climbing over. He lifts the covers, letting in a rush of ice cold air, and shunts me toward the edge of the sofa while he comes in behind me.

For I second I think it's a dead certainty I'm headed for the floor, but he quickly catches me with an arm around my waist and pulls me back in close to him.

"Jesus, Isla. What the fuck is this?" he chuckles, and the warmth tickles the top of my head. "You've got towels under here from arsehole to breakfast time."

What part of my outfit wasn't mangled by sleep has been mangled by the rearrangement, and I laugh because it's true. All the important bits are definitely covered, but, in achieving that, there are lumps and twists and runoffs all over the place.

"I don't even know how to start fixing it," I tell him.

"I miss the Rudolph suit," he mutters.

The underlying grumpiness in his voice somehow makes it more amusing. "Things you never thought you'd say lying in bed beside a girl..."

He chuckles, squeezing me around the middle, and it warms something inside me that's immune to external temperatures.

"Thanks… for the covers, I mean. And the body heat."

There's no response to that, only a sniff that heats and tickles the back of my neck in equal parts. He says he's cold, but he's not. He's warm. Roasting, in fact.

"Remember that night we met, and I told you if you won at pool, I'd take you wherever the fuck you wanted to go?"

I don't think I'll ever forget that night, so I nod. "Uh-huh."

"Well, that's me all squared up now. The debt's paid — you chose the sofa. Don't ever say I'm not good to you."

When I chuckle, he gives me another squeeze. And it feels… strange. Strange, but good.

I mean, he's still an arse, in my honest opinion. He's moody, and a bit too full of himself, and I suspect he thinks he's better than me. I also suspect none of that is actually personal — he thinks he's better than most people.

But the third thing I suspect is that somewhere beneath all that there is a half-decent human being.

And I'm thankful that right now, they're keeping me warm.

Chapter 9

Lewis

Isla Strachan is a fidget.

If she wasn't shoving her foot clean into my shin, she was digging her elbow into my ribs.

And the towels? The fucking towels? You ever slept in a washing basket? Nah, me neither. Until now.

And did the bony elbows, the freezing cold feet, or the two-hundred towels stop the wee man getting excited every time her arse got anywhere near?

Absolutely fucking not.

But as much as the wee man might like what he feels, getting in beside her last night was purely about staying warm. Last thing I need is her going all hypothermic on me when there's still a tree between us and the nearest hospital.

My head knows that, even if my cock doesn't.

I pull myself out from under the covers and dive off the sofa before she notices just *how much* the wee man doesn't deal in logic. The room is cold — even for me — but a cold shower doesn't seem like a half bad idea.

First, though, I need to get Kimber sorted out. She's pampered as shit only eats raw food, so the shortbread we had last night was off the menu. I plan to take her out this morning and let her have at it with a rabbit or a squirrel. Circle of life and all that.

I'm shoving my legs into my jeans when I hear Isla stir behind me.

"Can you see my breath? I feel like I can see my breath."

I turn around, adjusting myself and fasting the button on my jeans, and I don't miss her eyes move quickly from my bare chest to my face.

"All I can see is your hair," I tell her. I'm not lying — it's absolutely wild. She looks like she's been rag-dolled through a bush backwards.

She giggles and sits up, trying to run her fingers through the tangled mess and uncover some of her face.

"I can't hear the storm anymore?"

I cross the room to look out of the window. The wind has certainly died down, but the snow is still falling, maybe even thicker than it was yesterday.

"Aye. Seems to have passed."

"Do you think we'll make it out today?"

I shake my head. "Doubtful. It needs to melt some before we have any hope of moving that tree."

Crossing the room, I grab my shirt and put it on. "I need to take Kimber out — she'll be going stir-crazy stuck in here. I'll sort the fire and make coffee when I'm back, alright?"

She pushes the covers off herself, realizes her error when I get a full view of the towels' disobedience, and quickly does her best to rectify it while I spin around.

"I'll come with you."

I half turn, too momentarily surprised to remember why I had my back to her in the first place. "Catch yourself on." It comes out as words mixed with cynical laughter. "You can stay here."

"And do what, exactly? I'm decent by the way," she adds, starting up again before I've managed to turn around. "I'll go just as mad as the dog stuck here alone with no food and no heat and nobody to talk to."

"You think this walk is going to give you any of those things?" I lift an eyebrow.

I can see she's about to respond with *someone to talk to* but thinks better of it. "You don't need to respond to my talking."

I narrow my eyes.

"Or listen."

"Do you remember our little stroll yesterday?"

She puts her hands on her hips and sticks her chin out, all defiant. "That was different. You made me carry that big stupid axe — for no apparent reason, I might add."

I sigh and shake my head. I'd imagined a nice brisk walk with the dog — just me and my dog — and not spending the morning listening to Little Miss Are We There Yet.

"We'll take some coffee with us to keep warm. Maybe even some shortbread? For breakfast? It'll be like a picnic."

This a terrible idea. She'll be a nightmare. I can already see it clear as day in my head. But the defiance has somehow gone from her, and she's looking it me with those witch-doe eyes.

And I realize I don't have the heart to say no to her.

Well, the heart or the balls.

"Alright," I concede. "You make the coffee, then. I'm going for a shower."

She nods, fastening one of the six or seven towels around her chest and turning to make for the door.

"Isla?"

She looks back.

"What you gonna wear?"

Chapter 10

Isla

What am I going to wear indeed.

"I..." I look around, as if the poor person whose suitcase I accidentally stole is hiding behind the sofa and contemplating suggesting a trade. "I hadn't thought about that..."

He reaches a hand up to scratch the back of his head, and there's a part of me that wishes we'd had this discussion — and he'd had that reaction — *before* he put the damn shirt on. Then he holds that hand up.

I sense an idea on the horizon.

Hold my breath.

"I was thinking..." The hand goes down, and there's a pause long enough to warrant a little flicker of panic in my belly.

"You were thinking?"

He shakes his head. "Doesn't matter."

"Then say it with the knowledge that we're both aware it doesn't matter," I tell him, mimicking the way he said it last night and fighting the urge to put my hands on my hips because *I will* lose every single one of these towels.

"I keep a box stashed upstairs, things people leave behind. There might be something in there you could wear?"

Why, oh why, didn't we think of this yesterday? The smile almost cramps up the muscles in my face. "Lead the way."

He does.

I follow.

By the time we reach our destination, my head is manually sifting through the lost property boxes at the hotels I manage. I don't know what happens to the sunscreen, the first aid bags with those little sachets of infant painkiller that taste divine, or the knock-off Raybans. We only keep the good stuff. Electronics. Leather gloves. Coats and jackets.

Once glance, and I can see either Lewis doesn't get any good stuff, or if he does, he doesn't keep it.

Books. Magazines. Feather boas. Shot glasses.

My hand goes for the only thing remotely fabric like and I pull it out and hold it up in front of us.

It's red. It's sheer. It's the type of thing you put on for the specific purpose of taking off.

"Really?"

His eyes go wide for a second. Then a smile spreads across his face and he nods his head. Slow and cocky and deliberate.

"Really?" I repeat.

He tilts his head. "At least it's still got the tags on?"

Thank the lingerie gods for small mercies.

Chapter 11

Lewis

The wind has mostly died down by the time we leave the castle and head for the woods. It's still snowing, but it's not the full on blizzard it was yesterday — a fact I'm sure my little ice-box companion is pleased about.

Not that you'd be able to tell from looking at her. Every branch is loaded with thick white powder, and the ground is buried in feet of it, so one second she's screwing her face up and putting her hand above her forehead to shield her eyes from the burning brightness of it all, and then the next second the hand is dropping like a stone when she looses her balance.

You could say, *at least she's not dressed like a reindeer this time, Lewis,* but I'd be forced to ask if a hooker in hiking boots is actually an improvement. I mean, it's definitely just as comical, and since half the buttons are missing from the jacket, I get a fair eyeful every time the wind blows too hard and her hands are too busy shielding or stabilizing to preserve her modesty.

Not that I've got any business seeing — or thinking about — her modesty and what that little red number is doing to it. I took the cold shower to get any thoughts *remotely* in that category right out of my head. I'm still trying to figure out how well it worked.

Yesterday, well, she was just plain inconvenient, bordering on annoying.

Today she's still inconvenient, bordering on annoying, but there's a part of me — and I won't say how big — that can't help finding her fucking endearing.

Maybe I have a bit of that Stockholm syndrome. Technically *not* my captor, but I feel the principle of only seeing one person for so long that your dislike fades away and you start warming to them still applies.

I chuckle at my own thoughts and make it look like her latest tumble caused it, so she doesn't think I'm half daft.

Which I might be.

I mean, it's been twenty-four hours, Lewis. Pull yourself together, eh?

"Don't you worry that she'll get lost?"

She's talking about Kimber, who ran off into the woods in front of us about ten minutes ago and hasn't been seen since.

"What do you think she's going to do?" I chuckle. "Run away and join a pack of rabid wolves? She wouldn't last three hours before missing her old dad and coming back with her tail between her legs."

Isla laughs, but it comes out as more of a snort thing. "She calls you Dad, does she?"

I smirk. "All the time, darlin'."

"I'll believe it when I hear it," she says. "I'm just surprised you never called her Orkney or something."

It takes a second of confusion, but I do remember what she's referring to.

My shite chat-up-line about Islands and baby names from that night.

A lesser man might be embarrassed, but I own my shit and laugh it off, giving her a shove. "I was fucking smooth back in the day."

"Slicker than a boiled onion," she says with a laugh, attempting to shove me back and failing massively.

"Aye, well, it seemed to work on you, didn't it?"

"I was —" she stops herself, looking down before she can finish the rest of it. Some version of claiming her underage-ness as an excuse, no doubt. "I was... just about to say — at the risk of *you* saying *I told you so* — I'm exhausted."

There's a field just over the other side of these woods, and when I tell her the fence surrounding it would probably make a good seat, she likes the suggestion enough to follow me.

"It's like a babysitting a child, you know that, eh?" We're about halfway there and it's taken twice as long because she keeps stumbling.

"Are you always like this?"

I look down at her. "Like what?"

"Grumpy. Moany. Acting like your shoes are two sizes two small."

"Me?" I argue. "You're the one complaining all the time."

Isla scoffs, picking up the pace toward the field. Risky, considering her track record. "You told me I couldn't stay. Then you told me I *could* stay, but there was no fire, no heating, and no hot water. No food, no clothes, no feminine smelling body wash — which granted isn't your fault, but fairly sets the scene. Then you mimicked literally everything I said and did. I really haven't complained about even a tenth of that."

"You're complaining right now."

I'd intended that to be mildly witty, but she marches away shaking her head. She walks over to the fence and tries to push herself up, but with one hand trying to hold the coat together… she fails spectacularly.

If it wasn't for carrying her flask of coffee, I'd be stood with my arms crossed watching this entertainment for as long as she's willing to provide it, but I take pity and lift her up.

She adjusts her coat, and her lingerie, and her hair, and finally looks at me with a pasted-on smile. "Can you pass the coffee over, *please*?"

My feet remain planted a few feet away and I lift my chin. "Come and get it."

She pauses for a long second, and I wonder if maybe I've gone a little too far. I thought seeing her struggle to get down and back up on the fence would be funny. Comedy gold, in fact.

But I didn't want to upset the wee thing.

She looks over at the edge of the field like there's something over there worth looking at. "Fuck you."

Nope.

But I do it. I bring her the coffee and I stand next to her, leaning back against the fence and looking out over the field.

I wait until she's had a few sips before I speak again. "Is that you done with your wee outburst?"

She turns around and stares at me. "Is that you finished being awkward?"

I want to say something snide back, but there's not much I can say. Probably was being awkward. Probably been awkward since the moment she got out of that ridiculous Renault Clio. So instead, I just shove my hand out and gesture for her to pass the coffee.

"Come and get it," she tells me, rolling her eyes.

I push off the fence and take a couple of steps towards her. "Now who's being awkward?"

She pulls the flask back an inch, and not a ball-hair further because my hand snakes around it.

I'm standing near-enough right in front of her. A single step forward and I'd be right between her legs.

She doesn't let go of the flask.

I could pull it out of her hand like it's a bottle and she's baby… but she'd likely topple right off the fence.

I suspect she knows this.

Little Miss Are We There Yet is, yet again, testing my patience.

She raises her brows as if to ask me what I'm going to do about it, and I smirk at her.

Then her eyes move away from my eyes and rest on my lips.

I don't know the how and I don't know the why, but that little trick wipes the smirk off my face.

Her own lips curve up slightly at that, but she doesn't look away.

Eyes still locked on my lips. Hand still clamped around my flask. Breath still inches away from my cheek.

Now, I'm not going to pretend I'm any good at reading women. I have zero time for them and even less interest — not since I took a chance on a certain fair-haired temptress who gladly led me down the path of only narrowly avoiding a jail sentence.

That was ten years ago, and I've never felt the need to be wandering down any paths since then.

So while I've clearly been with women, I might not be the most experienced. But I have seen enough of *those* scenes on the TV to know that when someone's looking at your lips, there's a high percentage chance they want to kiss you.

That's always how it happens, right?

But that would mean she wants to kiss me.

Fuck would she want to kiss me for?

Maybe she doesn't. Maybe this is all just a big game to her. Wind him up and make him go in for a kiss just so she can laugh in my face when she asks me what the hell I'm doing.

Her eyes flick up to mine — probably to check I'm still watching her — and then settle back on my lips.

"Isla…" Her name comes out on a hoarse breath, and I fight the urge to clear my throat. What I should have done was asked her what she wants from me, but it feels like that would admit to what's going on.

And I'm not ready to admit to that.

Not if she's pretending. Pretending like she was in that pub on Christmas Eve all those years ago. Letting me think she's into me leading her on, despite her knowing nothing can happen.

Nothing real, anyway.

Nah. Nope. I've had my hopes crushed by her before, and I won't let myself walk into that again.

The way she's looking at me, though?

I expect it's not going to be easy.

Chapter 12

Isla

He's looking at me like I'm a juicy steak after days of nothing but dry shortbread.

His eyes are normally cold, and the only time they're not cold is when they're warmed by thoughts of tormenting me, but they're not cold right now.

Right now, they're warm and inviting and capable of drinking in a person's soul.

Just like they were that night.

And suddenly, I'm a teenager again. Knowing I should break this up, go back to the metaphorical *table-with-my-friends*... but I can't stop looking at him.

Something in his eyes makes me shiver, despite the lack of chill there.

The same undeniable, indescribable thing that kept me stood there joking about baby names and talking about island dates and thinking about deliberately losing a game of pool in the hopes of making both of those things a reality.

"Lewis…" I say his name for no reason other than the fact he just said mine.

My eyes drift over his face, taking in every inch of it from his thick eyebrows to his straight nose to his full lips.

I never got to kiss him that night, or if I did, then I don't remember, but I've thought about what kissing him would have been like often enough over the years.

I'm thinking about it right now.

Would his two-day-stubble scratch?

I hear a sound in the distance and I know if I look away, then whatever *this* is will be over.

And I don't think I want it to be over.

Not before I found out if *this* is even something.

But the sound is getting louder.

Closer.

He's dying to look away. I can see it from the way his eyes are searching my face.

Asking me what I want even though I don't know.

Telling me it's now or never.

Kimber.

The dog runs right between our legs and he takes a step back to make space for her. She's excited, bounding around between us and rubbing herself up against him.

"Someone's happy to see you," I tell him.

He chuckles lazily before bending down to clap her, and just like that… whatever the *something* was isn't there anymore.

"We should head back to the castle before you start getting all unbearable again."

Unbearable? I hop down off the fence and nudge him, but he just laughs me off with a swat and pulls the flask out of my hands. He takes a drink, still watching me while he does it.

"You know, you'd get way further with me if you tried being nice."

The words slip out of my mouth before I've even really processed what I've just said. What I've just insinuated — that he's trying to get somewhere with me. When he hasn't done anything *at all* to make any logical person think that.

What an absolute *tool* I am.

I start walking before he can notice the heat creeping up my neck and heading straight for my cheeks.

Footsteps in the snow behind me. He's following.

And he's laughing.

"I wasn't expecting to get anywhere with you. But now you've just admitted I could. Quite easily, too."

"I wasn't saying that," I shout without looking back.

"Sounded like it. Sounded like you just gave me the keys to the kingdom and told me to crack on."

"Really? Sounds like you're seriously confused." I look back now, trying to funnel those red cheeks into faux-rage instead of embarrassment.

I'll deny it until I'm blue in the face because I absolutely don't want him to think that I want him. Well, not unless I knew for sure he wanted me.

And I don't know that.

He's been a bit of a prick since the moment he set eyes on me. And maybe he has good reason to be, after what happened all those years ago, but whatever.

"It's alright princess," he says. "Don't fash yourself. Your secret's safe with me."

I roll my eyes, shaking my head as I stomp away.

If I've just turned him from moody and grumpy back to the cocky, cheeky man I knew years ago in the space of a single sentence, I'll find a way to move that damn tree myself.

I clear my throat. "I think we should get you home, *princess,* you know, before you go getting all unbearable on me."

He lets out a throaty laugh and grabs a hold of my hand.

I look down at it, half of me wondering what the hell he's doing while the other half is just pleased that he made a move — however tiny — and saved me from the cringe of being the only one.

Is this a move, though?

When I look up at him and he squeezes tighter, it definitely feels like one.

Chapter 13

Isla

"You know what's weird?" I tell him. "It doesn't even feel like Christmas Eve, you know?"

He turns around and lifts an eyebrow, resting his hands on the counter and leaning back slightly.

We're both in the kitchen waiting on the stupid tea lights to heat the stupid water for more stupid coffee.

I've realized this could be our life for the foreseeable.

Fifty percent drinking coffee and the other fifty percent waiting on candles to heat water so we can drink coffee.

Brilliant.

"What does Christmas Eve even feel like, exactly?"

He sounds skeptical.

"I don't really know… Like exciting and a little nerve-wrecking, but still magical, and just… Christmassy."

He chuckles. "Aye, maybe when you're seven years old, Isla. Not twenty-five and thirty-three."

"Och, wheesht," I scold. "You know what I mean. It's an atmosphere. It doesn't have to be a kids thing. Like that song about the drunk guy? I think he's in jail and his girlfriend is mad and he calls her a slut? What's it called again?"

"Feed the world?"

"No…" I tell him, shaking my head quite seriously until I realize he's joking.

He grins. "Oh, you mean Happy Christmas Yer Arse I Pray God It's Our Last by The Pogues?"

"Yeah that's it. No wonder I never remember the title."

He laughs. "That's not the title, darlin'."

"No matter," I reply, dipping my pinky into the water to see if we're beyond the lukewarm stage yet. Getting there. "It's not about the title, it's about the atmosphere."

"A bit drunk and a bit annoyed and a bit depressed and a bit naively hopeful Christmas Day is somehow going to be different?"

"No."

He raises an eyebrow, and I don't know, maybe he's right. No food, no music, no drink. No tree. You wouldn't even know it was Christmas.

"Do you have any decorations in the attic?"

His eyes go wide and he turns away quickly, checking the water even though I just checked it. "No."

"No?" Why do I feel like that's not the whole truth? Could it be because avoiding eye contact is absolutely the biggest telltale sign of a lie?

I inch my way over to him until I can see his face.

He's looking down at the tea lights, pretending like I'm not so close we'd be touching if we both took a deep breath at the same time.

"Lewis?"

"*Whit?*" he clips, turning his face towards me.

"Do you have decorations in the attic? And I'd appreciate an answer that's as accurate as possible."

He signs and turns around properly to face me. "I might. But we're not getting them down."

I stick a hand on my hip and eye him up. "Why not?"

"Because it's a shite idea. A shite idea that will involve me doing the work while you tell me it's not good enough. A shite idea that'll involve you fucking off the first chance you get while I'm left to put them all away again. How's that for accuracy, princess?"

"I'll do neither of those things." I shake my head and imagine the look on my face is extremely angelic while I stick my hand out. "Pinky promise."

He smiles and shakes his head right back at me, slowly. "I don't believe you. Plus, none of it's been touched since I was a sprog. There'll be spiders and cobwebs and squirrels and all types of beasties. You'll have a fit."

Hmm. Okay, so maybe he's right about that part. I'm not so keen on things that crawl or scuttle. Or just generally move.

But it would give us something to do that's not watching candles attempt to heat hot water.

"I'll be good. I swear." I tilt my head to the side. "Please?"

He looks up at the sky again, like the big man who's clearly not been listening the entire weekend is about to start now. He's not.

There's a sigh, and then his shoulders seem to relax and a butterfly starts flapping her wings deep inside me because I *think* I've got him.

"I hear you moaning even *once*, or see a look about you that alludes to similar, and I'm putting them all back."

I chuckle. "Cross my heart, hope to die."

"Stick a needle in my eye," he says, walking away. "I've a feeling that'd be more pleasurable."

I trail up the stairs behind him, reminding myself continuously about best behaviour. We take probably an hour to get the things down from the attic, and when I say *we* I do mean Lewis.

I offered to help.

Yes, it was halfhearted, but with the power being out and him having to feel around for things in the pitch dark, he said I'd do more harm than good if I went up there and I'm inclined to agree with him.

There was a minor disagreement when he found the tree and attempted to call it a day, but we compromised and he went back up for everything else.

"Right, that's your lot," he says, lumping what must be the ninth or tenth box down at my feet.

"Excellent, thank you." I grab the smallest one and make my way downstairs, hearing him follow on behind me. This one is light and feels almost empty.

Probably tinsel.

I've not had tinsel for years, and I'm mildly excited at the prospect of doing that thing with the paintings in the living room where you tuck it behind the corners and let the middle drape down.

I rip open the box (while he kindly goes back for the next one) and see that it's not tinsel at all, but those foil things that hang down from the ceiling.

Old school.

"These *always* make me want to sing that Boy George song, Comma-Charmeleon," I tell him when he comes back with another box.

"What?" he says, laughing while he puts the box down. He straightens, crossing his arms over his chest. "Fuck, Isla. You know it's not called that, eh?"

I turn around and lift an eyebrow.

"It's Karma. Why… why would it be Comma?" He screws his face up. "And what the fuck is a Charmeleon?"

"It's a Pokemon," I tell him. "The cute baby version of Charmander and Charzard."

"You've never — not once — wondered why Boy George would be writing songs about punctuation and Pokemon an entire decade before it was invented?"

I screw my face up. This… this makes no sense. "I don't mean comma like punctuation… I mean comma like someone's saying *come on* quickly. Come-on-Chameleon…" The look on his face tells me it's better for everyone involved if I change the subject. "Do you have a hammer and nails?"

He goes from staring at me like I've got two heads to staring at me like I've just asked him for a blood sacrifice in a split second. "Is there a reason you want to put holes all over my wall when sticky-tape would do just as fine a job?"

"You have sticky tape? That would do, I guess."

"Awfully kind of you, princess," he says, sarcasm so thick it's dripping.

It takes a couple more hours of sweat, sarcasm, and sacrifice, but by the time we've finished, the place actually looks lovely.

Better than lovely.

We've put the massive artificial tree in the alcove in front of the window, and even though the lights aren't on, the half-tonne of tinsel and giant red shiny baubles reflect enough light from the fire that it looks every bit as beautiful as it would be with them. We hung those Comma-Charmeleon foil things up from the roof, and I did the tinsel trick on every available painting and piece on furniture in the room.

"Now it feels a bit more like Christmas Eve," I tell him, standing back to admire our efforts. The light is almost entirely gone now, and my arms are aching and my stomach is past the stage of growling with hunger. But I feel better than I have in weeks.

I feel happy.

Weirdly excited.

Even though there are no presents, no friends and family, no fancy food or expensive drink. There's not even heating or power or hot water. There's just me and The Grinch, but somehow, that's okay.

"We're going to need to agree to disagree on that one, darlin'." He says. "It's not Christmas unless there's a whisky in my hand and the smell of something previously alive drifting in from the kitchen. Fuck your decorations."

"What you got against Christmas decorations, hmm?"

I eye him up and his face changes. Where before he was teasing and smirky, everything about him is suddenly straighter and a little more serious.

He looks around the room and swallows. "Nothing."

"Lewis?" I take a step towards him, and he looks down at the floor and gives me half a smile.

"Just memories, that's all." He shrugs. "Last time I saw all this stuff… well, my wee gran would have been right there in that chair with her knitting needles, pointing them at my granda' and threatening to shove them where the fire doesn't heat if he doesn't get more logs on it."

I smile, not saying anything in the hopes he continues.

"He'd huff and puff, muttering all sorts about her while we fetched more wood from the shed. And I remember trying to join in, like some sort of male solidarity or something, you know? He hit me with a stick," he says, chuckling. "*That woman's an angel sent from Heaven and don't you forget that you wee bastard.* It was only alright when he did it. Like, they'd bicker and peck at eachother, but they'd break legs if anyone else even thought about it."

"They sound great," I tell him.

"I miss them, this time of year." His voice breaks slightly in the middle, and I inch closer.

It feels like a hug would be the right thing to do, but he doesn't strike me as the emotional type. "I'm sorry," I tell him. And I mean that. If I'd known there was an actual reason for not wanting to pull all this stuff out that didn't feel like an excuse to dig at me, I would never have pushed so hard.

Surprisingly, he pulls me under his arm. A hug but not quite, and before I can think up a name to call it, he lets his arm slip, and it's over. "As long as the little princess gets to feel that Christmas atmosphere, eh?"

He's teasing, but he's not sarcastic this time. He's admitting that he's just indulged me, and it makes me smile. "Well, what's the Christmas atmosphere to you? Maybe we can fudge it…"

"You think there's a way to *fudge* whisky?" He lifts an eyebrow.

I screw my face up. "There wasn't a random bottle stashed up there in the attic for emergencies?"

"No such luck," he says, but his face changes quickly. "Wait there."

And just like that, he's out of the room before I can ask him what he's doing.

I take a seat on the sofa and finally shrug out of the jacket, arranging the blankets over me in an attempt to retain some dignity. A few moments later, Lewis returns, a bottle in one hand and a couple of glasses in the other.

"What's all this?" I ask, smiling at him despite myself.

"This," he says, holding up the bottle and winking at me. "Is what's going to keep me warm enough to spend another night next to your shivering."

Chapter 14

Lewis

"**W**hisky? No way!"

No way? This a twenty-eight-year-old bottle of Glenfiddich she's turning her nose up at.

"Just try it, Isla," I tell her, pouring us both equal amounts.

She shakes her head. "Honestly, I'm good. I don't drink that much at all. Not since…"

Her voice trails away to nothing because we both know what *since* is referring to.

"Well, you'll get no snuggles from me tonight unless you at least try it."

She laughs at that. She's laughing a little too much, considering it wasn't even funny.

"What?"

When she controls herself enough to speak, she shakes her head. "Nothing… it's just… hearing a man like you threaten me with *snuggles* is possibly the most preposterous thing to happen since I've been here."

"A man like me, is it?" I raise my eyebrow. "And what, exactly, is that supposed to mean?"

"I don't know," she says. "Just… a man like you."

I shake my head. "Is there no limits to the nonsense you spew on a daily basis."

She laughs. "I'll be talking even more nonsense if you make me drink that."

"Fine." I sit down on the floor beside the fire. "But don't you be sneaking in beside me tonight when you're frozen and I'm drunk and piping hot."

She eyes me up for a moment and then creeps down beside me, grabbing the drink from the table on her way.

"Jesus, that burns," she says, face looking like she's just been drop-kicked.

"You'll get used to it."

And that's how we spend the night — talking and drinking and laughing while she *gets used to it.* Even I can accept that the drink is going straight to my fucking head because my stomach's practically empty, so we grab the shortbread and get fired right into that.

"Are you feeling Christmassy now?" she asks. She's doing that thing with her mouth that tipsy people do when they eat, like it's the best thing she's ever tasted and she's well past caring about who knows it.

I chuckle at her. "I still don't know what I'm supposed to be feeling."

"Excitement." She shrugs. "Like bubbles and giddiness. Like the first night we met."

"Butterflies? You had butterflies the night we met?"

She smiles shyly and takes another drink. "You didn't?"

"Maybe wee ones," I concede. "Caterpillars."

She nudges me and puts on a gruff voice. "*Hi, I'm Lewis and I have a selective memory.*"

I have a selective memory? "*Nice to meet you, Lewis, I'm Isla and I keep forgot my own birthday.*"

She shakes her head and chuckles. "Are you ever going to let that go?"

I look down at my drink and notice it's empty, so I get up to pour another one. I know exactly what I want to say to her, but I can't be sure if it's the drink talking. Maybe some things are better left unsaid.

It was just yesterday I was telling myself there was no point in crying over spilled milk, and now I'm bitchin' like a petulant child.

"You're right. No point going over shit that means nothing anyway."

With that, she shifts her position and sits up properly. "What do you mean it means nothing anyway?"

I put the lid back on the bottle and rest it on the mantlepiece before turning around to look at her. She got too hot a wee while ago, just as I told her she would — what with the whisky — so she kicked the blankets off. And now she's sitting there in nothing but a tiny red nightdress.

The sight of her down there, a question on her face and the fire dancing across her skin, has a lump forming in my throat.

And it makes me angry.

Angry because of what happened.

Angry because of what *could* happen.

Angry because I know deep down that it can't.

She has a whole life. And her life is the whole fucking world. All I have is a dog and a crumbling castle full of ghosts and memories.

"I mean, there's not any point in bashing out the past. Not when we both have lives now and every intention of going back to them as soon as possible. It doesn't matter."

"Why didn't you ever call?"

Her question takes me by surprise because I really didn't expect her to push it after telling her to drop it. Then I scoff at it — as if the reason isn't obvious. "You weren't for me Isla, and you know it."

She shakes her head. "I was… *legal* that March. Three months. You could have got in contact then. You could have asked Gemma for my number, but you didn't, so you can't pretend I was some big heartbreak or something. You made zero effort."

I was a fully grown man, and she was a… baby. I still don't think she understands that. She thinks it's *no harm done*, but she wasn't there for the absolute roasting I got off everyone who saw us in the pub that night, everyone who didn't believe that the only thing I did was take her home.

She's still wrong, though. Even though I shouldn't have made an effort, even though it was seven levels of wrong, I did it anyway. "I asked Gemma about you," I argue. "She told me you were dropping out of school and going to college down in London in the summer. I wasn't going to put myself out there for you to leave this place like everyone else does."

I sit down beside her with a sigh and feel her eyes on me. Eyes which make me all sorts of uncomfortable. I've already said far too much, and we both know there's no going back from it.

"I didn't know that," she says, finally. "But maybe you're right, I guess…"

"I like you better with whisky," I tell her. "First time since we got here that you've told me I'm right."

She chuckles. "First time you've admitted you're capable of feelings."

I turn around and take in the sight of her, and can't help smiling when I see how pleased she looks with herself. "That wasn't me admitting anything, darlin'. Trust me, you'd know all about it if I did."

Her eyebrow perks up, and then she puts the drink down on the carpet beside her in the most deliberate way I've ever seen. "You keep denying it then. We both know that you know that I know."

I laugh at her minced words. "Can I have that in English, please?"

Chapter 15

Isla

I thought he was going to kiss me earlier on that fence. I really did. And now there is absolutely no doubt in my mind.

He wants me.

He's just scared to admit it.

And that's alright. I was scared, too. But that was before this magical thing they call whisky made me see things *so* crystal clearly. That was before he told me that he *did* at least ask about me.

And now I can't stop thinking about what would have happened if he *had* got in contact.

Would I still have left?

I don't know about that. Maybe if he'd tried. Who can say? I don't know anything for sure. But I *would* know what kissing him feels like, at least.

And now I really, really want to know what that feels like. And by the looks of him, so does he.

"I know," I tell him again, clearer this time.

"You know *what?*" he asks. He looks genuinely confused, and I don't know why, because it's all so utterly obvious to me.

It's Christmas Eve, just like it was that first night. That first night ended with me feeling too drunk, and him helping me into a taxi and taking me home.

Except the address he found on my driving licence wasn't technically my address, so I had to come clean that it wasn't my licence and it wasn't my age and it wasn't my star sign.

I don't remember exactly what he said. I remember him being angry and I specifically remember the words *jail sentence* being used at least twice.

It all ended with him dropping me off at my actual address when I finally remembered it.

And that was that.

I never saw or heard from him again, and then I left a few months later.

But we both knew what *should* have happened. And isn't it totally curious that we both ended up stuck here together on Christmas Eve, both a little drunk, both a little lonely, just like we were that night?

The only difference is that tonight we're both more than a little older.

"Maybe it was always supposed to be this way…"

Did I… did I just say that out loud?

I did.

Or the whisky did.

It was one of us.

He shakes his head, but he's still looking at me. And his eyes are hungry.

Why won't he just admit it?

I watch him swallow, his Adam's apple bobbing up and down, and it reminds me I really need to swallow too.

So I do.

Then I inch closer.

And then I look at his lips.

He just needs to *do it*.

"I don't want you doing something you're only going to regret in the morning," he says.

Why would I regret this? "I'm a big girl, Lewis. You don't need to tell me what I will or won't regret."

"It's been a long fucking time, darlin'. I'll not be able to stop."

"Then don't."

I say that like it's a dare.

He searches my face, maybe looking for a sign that I'm lying. That I don't mean what I say. He won't find one.

"I don't have anything." His eyes flick down to the space between his legs and I know what he's getting at. "Bad idea starting things we can't be finishing."

My reply goes through my head before I find the courage to say the words out loud. I know this is reckless. Stupid.

But I want him anyway.

Consequences be damned.

"I don't care."

"It's your funeral. What's another eighteen years of being stuck here with me, eh?"

I laugh at him, but he catches my chin in his hands before I can finish. I blink a few times before I sense he's actually waiting for an answer. "I can't think of anything worse."

He smiles. "I'll make every day torture. You can count on that."

I bite down on my lower lip. "What would you do to me?"

"Whatever the fuck I want to." He pushes my head back and comes with me, lowering me down on the blanket I had earlier.

"Sounds like a threat."

He lowers himself on top of me and takes some of his weight on his elbow, so I'm not completely crushed. His face is so close I can feel the warmth of his breath on my cheeks.

He smells just like he did that night… like mischief and leather and now firewood and whisky, too. Older. More complex…

"What if it was? What could you do to stop me?"

Taking each of my wrists in his hands, he pushes them up above my head and holds them there. Now his weight is on me completely and every breath is strained. Torturous.

"Nothing."

He smirks and traces his lips across my cheek.

A shiver of *something* runs down my spine and I squirm against his hard body.

This is hellish.

We haven't even kissed yet and already I feel like I need him.

Like every part of me is on fire.

"Say it again," he tells me, pushing his knee down between my legs and splitting them apart. "What could you do to stop me?"

His voice vibrates against my neck, and I swallow hard. "Nothing."

"I could keep you here as I long as I wanted." He presses his lips against my skin now. Finally. Gently and feather light. "I could keep you here forever."

"You could," I agree. I can't even think of a coherent response. I'm too dizzy, too lightheaded. Too needy.

His mouth trails back up across my cheeks until he's looking into my eyes. The light from the fire dances across his face, highlighting his bones and casting shadows on the dark side. "You should never have left, Isla."

I'm about to reply. My mouth is open, but whatever I was going to say gets lost somewhere between us. He captures my lips with his and suddenly I can't remember what I was going to say.

Agree?

Argue?

It doesn't really matter. Not tonight, at least.

All that matters tonight is finishing whatever this is between us. Finishing whatever we started *that* night, before everything went to shit.

His tongue works his way inside my mouth and it's exactly like I imagined it would be. Warm. Commanding. As if none of this is even a choice. As if it's the most necessary thing in the entire world right now.

He kisses me like he means it, and whether he does or doesn't is a problem for tomorrow to worry about. Tonight is for pretending this is real. Pretending we were written in the stars. Pretending we were always meant to be together.

I moan as he pulls away and bites down on my lip, and my hands struggle against his because I want to touch him. I want to pull that flannel shirt down his shoulders and run my hands over his muscles and feel him pressed up against me. The heat of his skin. The hair on his chest. The hard ridges of his stomach.

Everyting.

But he doesn't let me go. Instead, he settles his thigh up between my legs and pushes just enough for the pressure to send me grinding against him. His mouth moves to my neck, and every kiss is sheer torture, making my back arch and my hips flight against the sensation.

If I needed him before, then I'm desperate now.

"Lewis." I say his name on a sigh as he sucks harder on my neck.

Trying to break my hands free again, I wriggle some more and he finally lets me go. But it doesn't stop him. If anything, it only makes him hungrier.

I tug on the fabric of his clothes, desperately trying to get rid of them. He does the same with my nightdress, pulling it up over my stomach easily.

His fingers snake around my back, and I arch for him while he unclips the straps holding the bust together and slides the whole thing over my head.

Within moments our chests are pressed together, the hair on his against my nipples sending shivers of pleasure pulsing to my core.

His mouth covers mine again while he grabs my thigh and adjusts the position, and suddenly I feel my own wetness pressed up against the fabric of his jeans.

And then he moves.

Lower.

Kissing me the whole way. Hands exploring every inch of my body.

Without him on top of me, I feel exposed, the side of my body facing the fire burning up while the side pitched in darkness shivers from the cold.

"You're just how I always pictured you," he says, his hands cupping each of my breasts and kneading them. "Fucking beautiful."

I blush and close my eyes when his thumbs press down on my nipples. My thighs squeeze together around him, and I think I might possibly die if he doesn't fuck me right this second.

"Lewis… please," I whisper.

But still he doesn't. Won't. His mouth covers my nipple and as he swirls his tongue around, making my hips buck. It's like I'm not even in control of my own body anymore. He's the one pulling the strings, and I'm just dancing to his tune.

"Say it again," he says. "Tell me what you want." He moves across and repeats the motion, the cold air connecting with the wet trail he just left.

"I want you," I tell him. "Right now."

When he chuckles, I feel it in my fucking bones.

My hands run through his hair while he devours me, my nails trailing further down to his neck, his back, across his wide shoulders. "Please," I sigh.

Slowly, he shifts his weight back up, trailing kisses the whole way. His hand slides between us and undoes the button on his jeans. "I'm going to fuck you just like you want because it's been ten long years coming," he says. "But next time… next time, you're going to cry for it. Next time you're going to beg for it." Another kiss. "Next time you're going to need it like you need to breathe."

He positions himself at my entrance and I'm holding my breath while he works his tongue deeper into my mouth. I don't think he's breathing either.

It's like time is standing still.

Then he pushes in, all the way in, and lets out a low guttural sound, like it's painful for him.

"Fuck, Isla." He moans the words into my mouth while I squeeze my thighs hard around his body. His hands cup the sides of my face and the pressure becomes too much. I can't move. Can't think. I can barely breathe.

But still it feels so utterly right, and when he moves inside me, my whole body turns to liquid heat under him.

He's slow at first. Firm and controlled, even though I can tell he's holding back. I want to tell him he doesn't have to be. I want to tell him I can take it whatever way he wants to give it, but I don't think I'm capable right now.

I can't find the words, so instead I just kiss him and trial my fingers down the length of his back. Firm and controlled at first and then gradually harder… faster… more desperate.

My nails dig further into his skin and he moans right in my ear before slamming into me. I whimper from the shock of it, but this only seems to spur him on even more.

And now he's started, he can't stop. He drives into me harder, faster, until I can't even be sure of my own name. His hands curve around my ass, tilting my hips and pulling my whole body up closer to him until his cock is hitting places inside me I didn't even know existed.

The sounds that are coming from my mouth aren't my own… but neither are the ones coming from him. The more he does it — the harder he goes — the closer I get.

His fingers squeeze tighter against my ass and I cry out in pain… it doesn't stop him, though. Nothing could stop him. And I'm pleased because the worse the pain gets, the better it makes things… the more I inch closer until finally. Finally. I'm falling.

My whole body shakes as pure ecstasy rips through my body. His hands move up beneath me to my back and shoulders, wrapping me up and holding me tightly, squeezing me, and it's exactly what I need. I feel myself tighten around him as I come, and it's exactly what he needs too, because a moment later he squeezes me so tight I think I'm seeing stars. His cock throbs as heat erupts between my legs, warm and soothing and too perfect for words.

"Fuck, Isla," he says, before collapsing down on top of me.

I fight to get enough air in me while his chest rises and falls against my own. I'm hot, so fucking hot, but still I want him close to me.

He lays his head down on my chest while he tries to catch his breath and I lean towards him, planting a kiss on the top of his head.

My eyes close… I feel dopey and tired and *right*. So fucking right, like I'm whole. And it's the strangest thing because I've never felt like this before in my life, and I never expected to, either.

Finally, his breath steadies, and he shifts his weight off me. I feel empty for a minute, but he quickly pulls me back down on top of him, and now I'm the one resting my head on his chest while he kisses the top of my head and wraps his thick arms around me.

"So," he says, clearing his throat. "Was it worth the wait, then?"

I lift my head so I can see his face before I reply.

He looks… smug.

He knows what he did to me, the bastard.

I smile at him. "I refuse to contribute to your head growing any bigger than it is already."

He looks down. "Surprisingly smaller than it was five minutes ago, darlin'."

Chapter 16

Lewis

I think we must have fallen asleep on the floor in front of the fire, because I remember waking up in the middle of the night and having to carry her lazy naked ass up to the sofa.

Pretty sure we kissed, too. Just to keep the cold at bay. Obviously.

I wake up for real when it's still dark outside and untangle myself from her limbs, making a beeline for my clothes before I catch my death. The fire has long gone out, so that's the first thing I sort out, trying to make it toasty by the time she wakes up.

Then I do the usual. Let Kimber out the back, and light the candles to get the coffee started. I'm saying 'the usual' like it's the most normal thing in the world — and that's because, scarily, it's starting to feel like it.

I guess being stuck in one place with the same person and without basic necessities makes time feel different.

Which explains why what happened last night happened.

I mean, it was bound to happen, and if not, then it was definitely likely. We've had unfinished business for years, so adding alcohol and a major case of cabin fever to the mix was a recipe for disaster.

And by *recipe for disaster* I mean mistake.

Because we're clearly not going to be stuck here forever. She's going to leave. She has this whole damn life jetting all over the world, with her fancy hotels and high powered managerial job.

Even if I wanted to, even if *she wanted me to*, there's no way I could compete with that. I couldn't even manage to get myself out of this town, and I'm now I'm too old and too jaded to want to.

So, in hindsight, fucking her last night probably wasn't one of my brightest ideas. It took me more time than what's remotely healthy to get over her last time, and I thought about her way too much over the years, which is clearly ridiculous because nothing even happened between us. I was mourning something that didn't exist. Mourning the fantasy of her, not the real thing.

But now I've had the real thing.

And it was better than the fantasy.

I sit down at the kitchen table while I wait for the water to heat and tell myself — again — that I need to pull my shit together. She's leaving. Fucking get over it.

The only thing I can do is enjoy what time we have left together.

Then I can move on. Properly, this time. Force myself to meet someone, settle down, maybe have a couple of kids. All that good stuff normal people want when they're not hung up on ghost.

Kimber scratches at the door, and I get up to let her in. I'd thrown her out earlier without a second thought, but this time I shove my boots on. A wee bit of cold air will probably do wonders for the threat of a hangover.

Despite the darkness, the first thing I notice when I get outside is that it's not snowing anymore, and it hasn't been for a while. The second thing I notice is that it's nowhere near as cold as it has been, and the snow has melted considerably.

I bet if I took the car and the chainsaw down to that tree, I could have it chopped up and shifted before Isla even opened her eyes.

The thought of doing that has me feeling things I shouldn't be feeling. If I did that, there would be abso-lutely no reason for either of us to stay here. She could go to Gemma's, and I could go home.

And I'm a selfish bastard.

"Lewis?"

Her voice pulls me out of my thoughts and I turn around in the direction of the door. I can only vaguely make out her silhouette, the only light coming from the candles in the kitchen behind her and the faint glow of a low crescent moon.

I make my way over to the door and feel for her, my hand connecting with her bare shoulders. "Christ, woman, you're freezing. Get your arse back inside before you catch your death."

She has only the blanket wrapped around her, and her skin is cold to the touch. "I was worried when I couldn't find you," she says.

"What did you think? I'd done a runner?" I guide her over to the chair and cross the room to check on the water. "I was going to make you breakfast in bed."

"*Oooh*. What's on the menu?"

"Only the finest imported Italian coffee, otherwise known as Nescafe from the eighties. And a delicacy we call shortbread that's not stale, it's just *matured*."

She giggles. "You're too good to me, you know that?"

"Believe me darlin', we both fucking know that."

I make the coffee and we take the mugs and the last tin of shitey shortbread back to the living room, which has been heating up nicely. When this is all over, I reckon if a shortbread even thinks to look twice at me I will smash its dry face into a thousand tiny crumbs.

But for now, I'm too hungry to complain.

"Happy Christmas," she says, smiling. "Do you know I'd almost forgotten about that?"

I laugh at her — for all her moaning and pleading yesterday about needing the decorations up. "What, did I fuck the spirt of Christmas out of you last night or something?"

"Lewis!" She taps me on the leg and blushes, but her face looks amused enough to me.

"Well, someone had to mention it." No point in tiptoeing around it and pretending like it never happened.

"And you couldn't think of a single better way to slide it into conversation?" She takes a drink and looks up at me with a smile on her face. I look at her right back.

It's getting light outside. Won't be long before she looks out the window and sees how much the snow has melted. Before she asks me to go out and move the tree so she can get out of here.

Gemma will have heating and food and a warm bath. Gemma will have music and clean clothes and the Queen's fucking speech on TV.

I want to lock all the doors and close all the curtains so she can't see it. So she can't ask me.

But I know I'm just delaying the inevitable.

Maybe what we have now is just the same as what we've always had — a fun Christmas Eve and nothing more.

Maybe that was always the way it was supposed to be.

Or maybe Santa will be good to me this year and stick a wee baby in her belly. Then she would never leave.

I chuckle in my head — selfish little bastard.

"I'm going to get ready and take the dog out," I tell her. "You coming this time?"

She smiles. "Sure."

And I know that single word, right there, is the final nail in the coffin.

Chapter 17

Isla

The first thing I notice when we go outside is that Lewis takes my hand. No questions. No hesitation. He just grabs on to it like it's the most natural thing in the world to do.

As soon as I get over the shock of *that* is when I notice I'm not nearly as cold as I was yesterday. The thick white clouds of fog have cleared, and the low watery sun is clearly visible in the sky. The snow has melted enough to outline things on the ground now, and walking is definitely easier.

If we were walking in the direction of the road, the tree would be visible.

And if the tree was visible, we could cut the tree and move the tree.

And surely Lewis must have realized this.

But we're not headed in the direction of the main road and the fallen tree. We're walking the same way we did yesterday into the thick forest.

And strangely enough, I'm actually quite glad of that. I know I'm being stupid. I know I need to leave. I know I have a job and a life and a flight to catch on the 27th.

I know I need to leave... I just don't want to leave *right now*.

I want to indulge myself here with him and enjoy whatever *this* is. A Christmas fling, I guess, is what it is. And I need to keep reminding myself that it can never be anything more.

Even if I did the unthinkable and quit my job… what the hell would I do then? What next?

Live here with him?

He doesn't even live here, for starters. And even if he did, he clearly likes it better alone. Just him and his dog and his firewood. I imagine he lives somewhere secluded, maybe in a cabin or a little cottage by himself.

And me? I'm the polar opposite. I really hate being alone. In London, I have two flatmates who live with me. I have friends always dropping by. Sometimes I have to travel and spend nights alone in a hotel and I *hate* it with a passion.

Basically, I would do his head in.

We'd be so, so wrong for each other.

So why the hell am I letting my thoughts run away from me and imagining a scenario where this could maybe, *possibly*, work?

He probably wouldn't even want that, anyway.

We've been walking for what feels like hours in no real direction. You know, like when you're driving a car and you realize you have traveled ten miles closer to something, but you've no idea how you managed it? That's what walking while talking to Lewis feels like.

I'm not even aware of anything that's going on around me because I'm so focused on what he's going to say next.

I always knew he was funny since the first night I met him, but I also couldn't help noticing how much his light humor had changed over the years to dour-faced sarcasm. I can tell this morning he's trying his best to not be so cynical and I'm enjoying listening to him and the stories he has of growing up in this place.

When my stomach growls, I guess it must be near lunch. Shortbread doesn't keep you filled for long.

"We should have had the foresight to lay some traps or something… caught ourselves a wee turkey."

He looks down at me and lifts his eyebrow. "How many wild turkeys have you seen stoating around here?"

I smile at him. "Alright. Pheasant, then? I never realized how much I enjoyed eating birds until all I had was shortbread."

"The second I get home, I'm going to cook myself a whole chicken wrapped in bacon with a side of steak. Fillet steak, a big thick slab of it. I feel about half the fucking size I was three days ago."

Now it's me who's lifting my eyebrow. He *is not* a small man. "The shortbread cleanse was probably a blessing in disguise, if I'm honest."

He laughs. "Anymore of your cheek and I'll have to cleanse you right over my knee, darlin'."

"Is that a threat?"

He grins, and something moves in my stomach that's definitely not just hunger growls.

Chapter 18

Isla

By the time we get near to the castle, the sun has well passed the highest point in the sky. After he chased me for teasing him, caught me and put me over his shoulder to "teach me a lesson" we agreed we wouldn't last until tomorrow without food.

So he agreed to take the car and the chainsaw down the road and sort it out.

I didn't ask him what that meant for us, or if he'd go home tonight, or if he planned to take me to Gemma's house, because I didn't want to hear the answer. But I've spent the whole walk back to the castle thinking about it.

As soon as the trees clear enough for the castle to come into view, I realize I shouldn't have concerned myself with those thoughts.

I was worrying for no reason.

We have company.

"That's Jamie's car," he says as we emerge from the trees.

"Gemma's husband Jamie?"

He looks down at me and nods.

"But how did he get the car in?"

If Jamie can get his car in, that means I can get my car out...

Well, maybe not my shitty little city car. But definitely Lewis's big 4x4 Discovery.

It hits me that there won't be a repeat of last night tonight.

That was it. A one time only deal.

It makes me sad, but I tell myself I'll remember it forever.

"Jamie?" Lewis opens the door and calls out to him, but it's Gemma who appears in the kitchen, not Jamie.

"Isla!" Her face lights up when she sees me and she opens her arms out for a hug. She's lost some weight since I last saw her, and her dyed black hair has grown out from the short bob she had. I embrace her, breathing in the perfume that hasn't changed since we were teenagers. DKNY Delicious. Smells more like apples than apples do. "We didn't even know if you'd made it here — but then we saw the car. God, I've missed you!"

I pull back, grinning and showing all my teeth. I've seriously missed her, and it's only right now I'm realizing how much.

"We've been stuck here for two days," I tell her. "The power went out and we've had no heating and now we're out of food, too."

She looks from me to Lewis, who's standing behind me. "I've never known Lewis to deal well without food," she says, laughing. "But we're here now. We brought food, and Jamie sorted the electrics when we arrived — the power went back on through the night."

"Jamie moved the tree, too?" Lewis asks.

"He did, aye. Took him all bloody morning, too. Nice of you to help," she says, arms akimbo.

Lewis shrugs. "My fucking hero. Where is he anyway?"

"*Ben* the living room with Mya. So we'll be having none of that language—"

He's already walking away before she can finish.

I take a seat at the dining room table while Gemma finishes making the coffee. We still don't have any heating for the gas stove and a proper kettle, but we do at least now have some power, which is a relief.

"Please explain to me how you've managed to *not* murder him yet?" she asks as she hands me a cup of milky — *milky!!!!* — coffee. It looks so gorgeous and milky — milky! — and appealing that I don't give two shiny shits about the fact it's burning my tongue.

"Oh, he's not that bad, is he?" I say. The sarcasm in my tone so thick it's cooling the burned tip of my tongue.

She laughs and takes a drink of her own coffee. "I bet you were glad to see us. I honestly don't know how you coped. I said to Jamie this morning that it's colder in here than it is outside!"

"Well, the fire helped. It was the power being out that was the worst part. What I wouldn't give for a warm shower and a hot dinner."

She smiles in agreement. "Well, I spoke to the girls this morning — they've been staying in Edinburgh, but they're going to drive down today now that the roads are a bit better. They said to do dinner without them as it'll be dark before they get here, so let's finish this and then we'll send the boys out to the car for the food? Speaking of the boys, I don't fancy Mya's chances through there with her *half-wit* Dad and *dour-faced* Uncle. Are you coming?"

She stands up, and I follow her through to the living room. I had been wondering what she was insinuating — *surely they can't be that bad?* — but the moment we come through the door, I realize exactly what she's talking about.

I haven't seen Mya since she was just a tiny baby. I was working in Asia and since they had a tiny shot gun wedding, I skipped the party and came to visit the reason when she arrived. She must be three or four now, all strawberry blonde curls and an infectious laugh. And a baby she is not.

Lewis has a hold of her arms while Jamie has her legs, and they have her lifted between them like they're carrying a wheelbarrow, swinging her from side to side while they recite "*A Leg and a Wing*" and she giggles her little head off.

Gemma shakes her head and gives me a look that says, *see what I mean?* But I can't help smiling at them.

And that's how we spend the afternoon. Gemma and I worked with what we had and somehow got the turkey to fit in the old electric oven. We couldn't boil any veg — because of the lack of gas — but we got a good amount in beside the turkey.

The gravy, well, that was an absolute *shitemare* with the three-candle set up.

But finally, after what felt like hours of slaving away, we had dinner that on any other day would have been terri-ble, but today — after nothing but stale dry shortbread — Gordon Ramsay himself would struggle to find a single curse to utter about it.

And I can't berate the menfolk for leaving the cooking to us either. I think they worked harder than we did chasing Mya around the castle. Poor sprog was tuckered out and ready for nothing but a nap by the time dinner was ready.

"Merry Christmas," Gemma says, holding her glass up so everyone can toast. (We finally have the Prosecco I was promised and I am *more than happy* about that).

"Merry Christmas," I repeat, glancing at Lewis, who's sitting opposite, only to see he's looking directly at me.

I feel the heat rising in my cheeks, and I swear I'm trying everything possible not to make it noticeable. I feel sneaky, like we have some dirty little secret between us, sitting down for a nice family meal while the family-slash-besties are none the wiser.

Throughout the whole affair, we steal glances at each other. And I'm so torn. It's bittersweet. One side of my heart is fluttering every single time I lock eyes with him, only for that pesky thing called reality to sneak up with stomach-sinking boulders.

This is all going to be over.

And we didn't even get the chance to speak about it properly. Like idiots, we've both danced around the subject all morning — making jokes and teasing each other, which seems to be just what we do.

We never actually spoke about what will happen.

Will we stay in contact?

Will we see each other again?

But when Jamie stands up from the table at the end of the meal and announces they should leave us to our girly Christmas, I swear my stomach falls through the floor because I already know what's coming.

The girls will be here soon, and the boys will scarper.

It's funny because this is exactly what I wanted when I came here, and now I think it might be the last thing I want.

Lewis stands up too.

"Aye," he says, nodding his head. "Kimber needs a proper feed, and it's getting late."

I swallow, and then nod my head because I think my face might betray how I'm feeling — and I really don't want it to.

Gemma gets up and starts clearing the plates away. Jamie goes over to the sofa to fetch a sleeping Mya.

Lewis approaches and looks down at me for a moment without saying anything at all.

"I guess this is it, then?" I say. The question was rhetorical. I just couldn't stand the silence any longer.

"Aye," he says, nodding his head slightly and then checking we're out of earshot. "I guess this is it, princess."

I swallow. I'm not really sure what else to do. I thought he was checking if we were alone so he could say… something. Anything.

Obviously not.

"Well… thank you, I guess."

The hint of a smile plays on his lips, and after a few moments, he replies. "Thank you, too. *I guess.*"

Then he nods his head and walks right by me.

I turn around and watch him leave.

Gemma comes back, and I quickly straighten myself and put a smile on my face. "More Prosecco?"

"Of course!"

She pours us both another glass as Lewis and Jamie head out the front door.

And I have that sinking feeling in my stomach. I'm trying to think of something to say, anything that will take my mind off it…

"I wonder what time the girls will arrive?"

"*Uugh*, let me grab my phone and check," she says, crossing the room to the smaller sofa where her purse is sitting.

"It's no use," I tell her. "No one gets a signal here."

"Nonsense," she says. "You just have to be selective about what networks you choose." Her face lights up as she unlocks her phone and fiddles around with it. "They're an hour away, and that was twenty minutes ago."

"So… forty minutes then?" I tease.

"Forty minutes. Just enough time for you to explain why you were eye-fucking my cousin over the table during Christmas dinner?"

My eyes go wide. "What?"

She raises her eyebrow and plops herself down on the sofa beside me, tucking her legs up under her. "Don't give me that innocent face. Spill. And leave *nothing* unspilled."

Chapter 19

Lewis

Kimber jumps in the boot of the car, and I strap Mya into the back seat while Jamie sits on his arse doing the square-root of fuck all. Apparently, that's only fair since he spent his entire morning clearing my road and sorting out my electric.

Not that I asked him to.

If he hadn't bothered, I'd still be in there with Isla. Probably starving, but also probably naked, which is a price well worth paying, in my humble opinion.

Slamming the door shut, I fish my keys out of my pocket and start the engine, wincing at the feeling of the ice cold leather on the steering wheel.

"Fucking *baltic*," I tell him.

"Gemma will have your balls for earrings if she catches you speaking like that in front of the wee hen. But aye, you're right — it's not half getting colder again."

I turn around as I reverse the car out and see Mya's distracted, half turned around in her seat, trying to convince Kimber to jump over the rail so she can play with her.

"Can't think of the last time I never had a drink on Christmas night," he says, glancing back at Mya when she does her best attempt at a bark.

I chuckle. "I'll be thinking of you singing *Twinkle-Twinkle* while I'm getting fired into my whisky with the dog sleeping at my feet."

He shakes his head. "Prick."

"Language," I scold.

We drive down the long track until we reach the tree, which he's cut up and piled at the side of my road. "Couldn't even stack it properly," I tell him, tutting under my breath.

"I'm an electrician — not a fucking tree whisperer like you. I think I did an alright job. You should be down here kissing my boots."

"Away and shite!" I'm shaking my head but laughing too.

"Don't tell me, you were quite enjoying yourself being locked up there with your childhood sweetheart."

I turn around and screw up my face. "Childhood sweetheart, is it?"

"Aye. She was a child, and gave her your heart."

I punch him in his arm, but he's killing himself with laughter now. "That's shite-talking and you know it."

"Alright, alright. Maybe that was below the belt. You must have tried with her, though, surely?"

This time I don't look at him.

I keep my eyes firmly on the road.

Jamie is probably the best friend I've got. We grew up together, shared everything. Hell, I guess we're family. When everyone else left for the cities, it was only him and our friend Dean who stayed.

But that doesn't mean I'm going to start talking about feelings and shit.

"Lewis?"

"*Whit?*"

"You're avoiding the question."

"Nothing happened," I say.

He chuckles and shakes his head before looking out of the window. "You're just going to let her walk away again."

"What are you talking about?"

He scoffs. "I saw the way you were looking at her. You fucking like her, don't deny it. And what I'm saying is, don't be a stubborn, silly bastard like you were ten years ago."

I roll my eyes. If it was as simple as he's making it out to be, then maybe, *maybe*, I would swallow my pride.

But it's not that simple.

It's pointless.

She has a life. A good one. One that's better than anything I can offer her here with me.

Chapter 20

Lewis

It's easy to deny shit when you're in defense mode.

It's a harder thing entirely when you've been sitting on your sofa for an hour doing nothing except staring at a wall.

Don't even know why I'm staring at it.

Don't know when I started.

Don't know why I've not stopped yet.

All I know is I feel restless. Which is really nuts, because I'm doing exactly what I *would* be doing any other night. I usually fall asleep like this after dinner and stumble through to bed in the wee hours.

It's just never felt this lonely before.

"What you looking at me like that for?" I say to the dog. She's doing that thing where she's got her face between her paws low on the ground. Her tail begins to wag the second I open my mouth.

I often wonder what dogs would say if they could speak. They're always so fucking happy to help — like you can't even open a cupboard without them coming to lend a hand. Would she tell me to stop being so fucking stubborn? Or, maybe, she likes it better just me and her. Dad all to herself.

The way it's always been.

She was brooding, though. She *is* brooding. Just like me.

Thing is, though, there's nothing I can do.

I can't go back over there and make a scene — not while my cousin and all her friends are there. What if Isla told me to leave? I'd never live a thing like that down in this town. I've barely lived the last Christmas Eve with her down.

And I didn't even get her number, so it's not like I can text her. And even if I did, even if I could, she doesn't get a signal there anyway.

But… she would get a signal in London, wouldn't she?

I wonder if I could find her on that thing. What's it called again… Facebook? Are people still on Facebook?

The dog gets a fright when I stand up suddenly, and she follows at my heels on the way out to the car. See what I mean, always trying to help. I grab my phone for the first time in days and plug it in.

This thing is usually just an expensive watch, as that's all I use it for, but it *does* have the internet. Somewhere. When it finally turns on, it vibrates in my hands.

Gemma.

Likely from this morning. Or maybe even the day before.

I open up the conversation, and I'm about to start at the start (there are more than a few) but my eyes are drawn to the last cluster, and one word specifically.

Isla.

19:46

Hey. It's Isla. This is going to sound crazy, but… I don't want to leave things the way we did. If you do, then that's totally fine, of course. I mean, if it was a one-night thing, then that's cool. But I just wanted to let you know it doesn't have to be…?

20:58

God.

Oh god.

Just forget I sent the last message!

22:02

Said id giv u to 10pm but think its Drikn talkinnn

Byew Lews Xx

I swallow.

Hard.

She text me and I didn't even know.

Stupit bastard.

I begin to type a message back, basically apologizing for not seeing it and letting her know I don't want to leave it the way we did either. It feels like unfinished business, and I've already lived too many years of my life having unfinished business with Isla.

I don't want to do another ten.

But I quickly realize that's a stupid idea and delete the message before I can send something I'll regret.

Replying to that message would be stupid.

I've been stupid.

I won't be stupid again.

Chapter 21

Isla

"Still nothing?" Jess asks.

We're all sitting on the sofas around the fireplace, in our Christmas pajamas (thanks to my now dry reindeer onesie) with our Prosecco in our hands, just like we all intended. Louise and Jess brought more shortbread, but I told them to keep it the hell away from me.

"Nothing," I tell the group.

I can feel my voice slurring a wee bit. I'm that way where I'm *fine* — I mean, I'm not sicky or spewy or anything — but the room isn't quite as straight as it should be. I can't even text him again because:

A) I think I might have fucked the last one up and…

B) no one likes a desperado.

"I know what he's like with phones — absolute liability. Also, I've never known Lewis to stay awake after nine. I'm sure he'll reply in the morning," Gemma says.

I've been sitting here cradling her phone like it's my baby for hours now. Maybe she's right, but I don't want her to be. It's Christmas night, and even if it wasn't, being here without him just doesn't feel right.

It feels empty, even in a room full of people.

"Does he have a house phone I could call?"

It takes me a couple of seconds to realize they're all laughing at me. "It's our duty to you, as your best friends, to make sure you *definitely* don't do that," Louise says.

"Yeah, I mean, the *third* text explaining why you sent the second text was already too far," Jess says with a giggle.

"He doesn't have a house phone, hun." Gemma pats me on the thigh and I smile at her.

It might be the drink talking — in fact, it's *definitely* the drink talking — but I get the idea I should just go there.

Getting up from the couch like I've found a new lease on life, I plop my glass down on the table with unsteady hands and look around the room, trying to remember what the hell I did with my shoes.

"Gemma, phone me a taxi," I tell her, throwing her mobile at her. "And also, tell me his address."

When I first sent that message, I wasn't sure if any of this was the best idea. But now I know it is.

They're about to protest and I put my hands up. "Fuck the flight on the 27th. Fuck work. Fuck my pokey little shoe-box apartment in London — the guy lives in a goddamn castle. In fact, fuck this castle, too. I'll live in a hut if it means being with him. Do you hear me? I'll live in a hut!"

We'll make it work.

Hut or no hut.

But I need to tell him this.

It's practically bursting out of me.

"Woah there, lady," she says, half of her apparently laughing, the other half — the face half — looking increasingly worried. "Maybe we should all sleep on this, and if you still feel this way in the morning, I'll take you there myself."

"I can't sleep on it. Christmas will be over! Don't you understand? It's the Prosecco that's letting me see inside my true heart."

I glance over at Jess and Louise, who appear to be killing themselves laughing. They don't understand.

Nobody understands.

"That's *exactly* why you need to sit yourself down," Louise says with a giggle.

"It's Christmas Day, Isla. You'll be waiting for a taxi until the cows come home…" Gemma says.

"I can't." I shake my head. "I can't stop thinking about him. It's like my chest feels physically sore. Either I'm getting in a taxi or I'm walking, but I *am* going to his house — or his hut — and I *am* telling him exactly how I feel."

"Sit your arse down, stupid woman."

We all turn around at exactly the same time.

And I don't know if my heart is soaring with delight at seeing him, or if I'm dying from the shame of *him* seeing *me*.

So, I sit down. Just like he told me to.

I look from Lewis to the others, and we're all just looking at each other.

"Hi Lewis," Gemma says.

Thank god.

"Hi Gemma," he replies, but he's not looking at her.

He's looking right at me.

"Isla, will you help me with something in the kitchen? Please."

His face is straight and stern looking, and I look around the group — what exactly I'm looking for, I do not know.

Reassurance that he didn't hear my hut speech and that the hut speech wasn't as bad as I'm remembering it, maybe?

Finding absolutely none, I stand up from the sofa and follow him out of the room, feeling kinda like a school girl walking to the Principles office.

He caught me saying that.

How much of *that* did he actually catch?

That's the question.

And there is no obvious answer.

I want to curl up into a ball and… well, we get to the kitchen before I can choose what, specifically, I want to do once I'm in that ball, but it's either die or cry.

He turns the lights on and then goes over to stand at his usual place over by the counter.

I'm about to perch myself on the little seat, like I've done so many times when I've watched him heat water with three candles.

But he doesn't give me the chance to sit down.

He takes a hold of my hand and pulls me towards him, positioning me so we're chest to chest.

I look up at him, waiting for him to say something. I mean, it's clear he wanted to talk to me, right?

Probably wanted to let me down gently.

He doesn't say a word, though.

Instead, he just stands there staring at me for long seconds.

After a while, I can no longer fight the urge to explain myself.

"Lewis, I wanted —"

"*Shhh...*" He cuts me off with a finger over my lips. "I think we've heard just about enough from you tonight, darlin', don't you?"

I smile beneath his finger. He probably heard more than he should have, but still, I can't help wanting to mitigate the damage, so that if he doesn't feel the same way, I can somehow get myself out of it.

"First of all, I didn't text back because my phone was in the car. Second of all, if you'd walked to my house — not hut — in the middle of the night in this weather, I think I would have strangled you on sight. And third. Third. Tell me what to do now because I can't fucking let you go, Isla."

I search his face, looking for a sign that this is some sort of sick joke.

Does he really mean that?

Has he had prosecco too? And if yes, does the prosecco make him truthful like it does me, or does it make him a trickster? A joker?

Could that be possible?

His finger drops from my lips, but I don't know what to say.

I need to know.

"Are you…?"

He nods before I can ask him if he's being truthful.

When I realize I believe him, something lifts in my chest. I don't know what it is… it's like the boulders, the pebbles, the little rocks, but it's not sinking.

It's lifting me higher than I've ever been before in my life.

But even the truth-serum prosecco isn't strong enough to keep reality out much longer.

"I don't know… I don't know how it's going to work, Lewis."

As much as I want it to, he needs to know that it's not like I can just pop up and visit on the weekends.

I live on the other side of the country.

I work all over the continent.

I can't just come for the odd sleepover — as much as I'd want to.

If we're doing this, it has to be…

"I don't know either but the less I'm giving a fuck," he says, shrugging. "You're not leaving me again. I won't be able to live with myself. If that means I need to figure out how to get a passport and —"

I shake my head, cutting him off, unable to hide the smile that's working its way across my face. "No. I don't want to leave."

He smiles now too. "Well, that's good, cause it wasn't even an option. I'd lock you in this castle until the day we die. The passport was a fallback, in case you ever escaped…"

I laugh at him. He's joking, right?

Chapter 22

Lewis

"Come on… I'm taking you home."

I take her hand, about to lead her to the door, but she digs her heels in.

"I can't leave," she says. "What about the girls? Chicks before —"

"Do you want to find out how easily I can pick you up and give you the word you were about to say?" I ask her with a shrug, only half-joking.

"Let me tell them, then."

She slips out of my grasp, and I head out to the car to wait for her. It's well below freezing and pitch dark out here, the only light coming from the flickers of fire escaping through the windows in the living room.

I watch the figures from the window while leaning against the car. I'm glad I didn't mess about with knocking on the door and waiting for a reply. Walking in like I did, and hearing her say what I did, saved a whole lot of time. She would have just denied shit and danced around the issue, like we've both being doing for days. Years.

But she can't deny anything now.

I see her figure appear in the shadows and unlock the car, walking around to get the door for her. Before she can jump in, I take her by the shoulder and push her up against the side of the car, boxing her in with an arm at each side.

She looks like she's about to say something, but I don't let her. I don't want to hear it. She can say all she wants to say in the morning over breakfast. She can say all that when I'm finished with her.

My mouth covers hers and she takes a second to react, but when her mouth gives me an inch, I take the whole fucking mile. My cock stirs instantly, already craving the feeling of her wrapped around it, and I push myself up against her while she lets out a soft sigh.

I slip my hands down, grabbing the back of her thighs and lifting her up so I can bring her closer to me. What I wouldn't give to rip that daft reindeer suit off her right now and fuck her against the car, and the second she lives with me is the same second she never wears Christmas pajamas ever again.

I'll rip every single pair she owns right off her body if I have to.

"Lewis, take me home," she says through the kiss.

Right.

Home.

There's time for all of this later.

I let her slip down my body and then help her up to her seat, before getting in myself and starting the engine.

The roads are awful again with the temperature dropping so much that it's turned the melted snow back into ice, so I'm trying to drive slowly and carefully, but all I can think about is getting home and burying myself deep inside her.

At least, that was the plan.

By the time we arrive at my house… Isla has a different idea.

She's fast fucking asleep.

Too much of that sorry excuse for champagne she drinks.

I get out of the car and come around to her side, unclipping her seatbelt while trying not to wake her. Then I slide her into my arms and lift her out of the car. She stirs a wee bit, before finally resting her head on my chest and going still again.

There will be no burying of the wee man tonight.

So I take her up the stairs and tuck her into bed.

I meant what I told her earlier… I have absolutely no intention of letting her go. I can let the woman sleep in peace for one night, at least.

Chapter 23

Lewis

sla Strachan is a fidget.

Aye, aye, we discovered that a wee while ago, didn't we? Don't care. If I have to be reminded of it every last-thing-at-night and every first-thing-in-the-morning, then I won't be judged for mentioning it.

She's a fidget in the sheets, helpless in the streets (okay, the forest), and an even bigger pain in my arse than the daft dog… and still, every morning waking up next to her, I realize I like all of those things more than I ever thought possible.

I like being booted in the thigh in the middle of the night. I like that sorry little face when she insists on taking the dog out with me, the one she pulls when she regrets it eight minutes later. I like having to think about what I'll cook for dinner because she's not a total carnivore. I like having to think about the fact there's no milk for the morning because she needs it for her porridge. I like having to think about not leaving the toilet seat up because if she finds that in the middle of the night, she'll probably fall right down the pan.

I like every annoying, helpless, pain in the arse thing about her.

Is that witchcraft, do you think?

Don't know. Don't really care, either.

It's the thirty-first of December. Hogmanay. She had me at the store this morning with a list of 'party food' and 'nibbles' so long that I half suspected a hidden cock-confetti on the agenda somewhere in the middle. Once she caught wind that Jamie likes to set off fireworks for the bells, but not this year because Mya got a pony for Christmas, there was no stopping her.

Why don't we do it at the castle?

Naturally I said yes, because I somehow lost the ability to say no to her within twelve hours of seeing her again, and here we are.

Gemma's parents. Jamie's parents. Some of our old friends and their parents. Word spreads and before you know it, you have the entire town hall, including the vicar and your old headteacher, sitting in your living room getting drunk.

But she's happy, and it's past the twenty-seventh and she's still here, so who am I to moan about the means when I'm more than happy with the ends?

"Lewis! There you are!" She comes out from the kitchen dressed like she's coming out a nightclub. All glitter and sparkles and big hair. We drove up to Edinburgh a few days ago, both to return the *Clio* and because neither of us could function with her walking around the house all day in nothing but my t-shirts, and I reckon I'll be discovering the fruits of that shopping trip long into the springtime.

I like this one.

The wolf whistle lets her know that.

She taps me and shakes her head. "There's still a tray of mini-pizzas and two lots of sausage rolls in the oven barely cooked — what time is it?"

I check my watch. "Eleven minutes 'til the bells, darlin'. Have you been in that living room recently?"

She shakes her head. "How comes? We've been in the kitchen… with the punch bowl."

The way she whispers the last part and the guilty look on her face makes me want to kiss her, but it's quickly replaced with a frown when she remembers the food versus fireworks dilemma.

"*How?*" I repeat. "Because I doubt there's a soul left through there sober enough to notice the difference between a frozen sausage roll and a charcoaled one. Just leave them. Grab your coat and I'll start herding people outside."

She lifts herself up on her tiptoes and I give her a kiss before we go our separate ways. Eleven minutes to locate Jamie, find out where he wants everyone, and get everyone from in here to out there before making sure she's back at my side for the stroke of midnight and the accompanying kiss.

I'm a ball-hair away from going full on *guy-from-titanic* when the first class folks won't stop messing about with their champagne and their orchestras, they won't put their lifebelts on or go anywhere near the boats and the Irish guy starts taking matters into his own hands — and I know all this because apparently they always show it at Christmas except *this year* Isla made me sit through all three hours of it… but thankfully it doesn't come to that.

She's by my side just as the crowd starts the out-of-sync count of *ten.*

I twirl her around toward me and lift her chin with my finger.

Nine.

"You're staying, then?"

She's still looking up at me when *seven* happens.

"I'm staying. Cross my heart, hope to die."

Stick a needle in my eye.

I want to kiss her right now, but it's too early.

Five.

It would ruin the moment.

If I kissed her right now.

Wouldn't it?

Fuck it.

It's *two* when I pick her up and wrap her legs around me. The first bangs start, but her hands are covering my ears, cupping my head and my face and pulling me in closer. I feel the fireworks in my chest like the thudding of my heart — her heart — both of them together.

And when her lips catch mine and the crowd around us erupts, that's when it hits me.

This year is going to be different.

Very different.

And I have no idea how different or what that means, but I genuinely can't wait for it.

Epilogue

Isla

I wave goodbye to the last guests of the season and breathe a sigh of relief as I get into the car. It's six o'clock on Christmas Eve, which is a late check-out for sure and something I should have never agreed to, but well, I'm a softie and it's Christmas. That sigh of relief signified the fact I'm more than ready to go home, get my pajamas on, and curl up on the couch with a glass of Prosecco.

It's been a challenging year for sure. Opening up a hotel and working out the inevitable kinks has taken up more time than I planned for. But things are good now. Much better than last year, when I couldn't even have a glass of Prosecco after days like this.

She was worth it, though.

I jump out of the car and can already see them all through the big window at the front of the house. When I think back to that night when I decided to stay… the castle might have played a minor role in the decision-making process. Of course I meant what I said about having him in a hut if that's what it took, but really, who wouldn't want to live in a beautiful centuries old Scottish castle surrounded by trees with a bed that has *actual stairs* leading up to it and its own (perfectly safe, I found out) Juliet balcony?

Well, that was before Lewis took me home to his actual house, which turns out is the polar opposite.

Nestled in woodland, but still only a mile away from the town, it's like a little sanctuary. A modern sanctuary. So white it practically shines in the low winter sun, with almost as much glass as there are walls.

I must admit I laughed when I discovered his whole "I sell firewood" thing was the understatement of the century. Yes, he sells firewood. He just failed to mention he owns the whole damn forest from here to the castle, too. And in a place like this, firewood is as much a necessity as bread and milk.

Technically, we could have earned nothing from the castle and still been alright. But it would have been such a waste, and it created the ideal passion project for me. It's not been easy — we restored and refurbished almost everything while I was pregnant with Skye — but now it's done. And business is doing better than I could ever have hoped for.

"Mum's home!" I hear his overly excited voice drift in from the living room and a few moments later, the patter of tiny feet on the tiles.

"Oh, I missed you," I tell her, scooping her up in my arms and taking in a deep breath of her. She's one now, so she's losing that baby smell they all have, but there are still traces of it.

A few moments later Mya comes too, to see what's going on. She's incredibly protective of her wee cousin, and the pair of them follow each other around like shadows. I put Skye down and Mya lifts her up — something I've told her not to do countless times because I fully accept I'm that annoying precious firstborn mother — and makes her way back to the living room.

Lewis is sitting on the floor in the middle of a train set, while Gemma and Jamie are on the sofas with a cup of tea in their hands.

I'm betting Gemma made those, as Lewis's hosting skills have not really improved in the two years we've been married.

"Time d'ye call this, woman?" His tone is stern, but his face is teasing.

"Well, someone has to graft while you lot sit around all day. Make yourself useful and get the kettle on." I nod towards the kitchen and he shakes his head slowly, then gets up anyway, stopping on the way to plant a quick kiss on my cheek.

I collapse onto the sofa and take my boots off.

"That you all done for the year now?" Jamie asks.

"No guests til the fifth of January and I could not be more happy about that," I tell him.

He laughs.

"Oh Isla, did you remember to pick up the tatties for tomorrow?" Gemma sits up, almost panicked looking, and I smile at her.

"They're in the car with the drink. Lewis'll bring them in later."

She lets out a breath of relief and then gets up. "Right, we best be getting home then, get the wee one to bed," she says, then lowers her voice to a whisper to add "and Santa still has a bike to build."

We both glance at Jamie, and he rolls his eyes before he gets up. They say their goodbyes — shouting through to the kitchen for Lewis — and then I start our little Christmas Eve routine with Skye.

We have matching pajamas. Yes. We are that family. Matching pajamas, hot chocolate, cookies and whisky for Santa-slash-Lewis, and a carrot to put outside for Rudolph.

Then we watch the snowman, and Lewis reads her *The Night Before Christmas* before taking her to bed.

When he comes back down the stairs, I already know what he's going to say before he opens his mouth.

"Right darlin', time to get those Christmas pajamas straight to fuck."

I giggle because I was right, and because his face is actually deadly serious. Shaking my head slowly, I reply, "We had a deal and you know it."

"You used Skye against me for that deal. It was underhanded and poor patter from you."

I smile at him while he kneels down on the floor at my feet. "A deal is a deal. Is it even Christmas if I'm not wearing Christmas pajamas?"

He lifts an eyebrow. "Is it even Christmas if I'm not ripping them off you and fucking you into the rug?"

I almost spit my tea out. He's right though. It may or may not have become somewhat of a tradition.

"We've got all night for that!" I argue.

He shakes his head, his hands coming up my calves and tracing circles on my thigh.

"I'm Santa now — I've got a dollhouse to build and at least a hundred batteries to fit. But I'm not an unreasonable man… I'll give you another deal?"

Now I'm the one lifting my eyebrow. "And what deal is that? You want to beat me at pool again?"

He chuckles. "Nah, too easy. I'll give you the carrot instead of the stick this year…"

"Spit out the deal before I take that carrot and use it as a stick on you."

He laughs. "Right, the deal is simple, darlin'. You fuck me now, and I read the instructions for the dollhouse. You make me wait, however, and I go in blind and do it myself."

It's so fucking ridiculous I can't help laughing at him. "You are one twisted little man."

"Little?" His hands reach up further, diving towards my waist and pulling me closer towards him. I almost spill the damn tea. "Little?"

"Little," I say.

He takes the mug right out of my hand and puts it down on the floor beside him. "You could have had the carrot, Isla. Now you're getting the stick."

I'm about to argue, but his hands are already wrapping around my head, pulling me closer so he can catch my lips. My argument would have been pathetic anyway... considering I want it just as much as he does.

The moment his lips meet mine and he drags me down onto the floor on top of him, the argument for putting this off makes absolutely no sense.

His hands are everywhere, pulling at my beloved Christmas pajamas and sliding them over my head.

The first time we did this, things were less than perfect. We had no power, no food, no beautiful twinkling lights on the Christmas tree like we do now. We had no idea if this would ever work out. We didn't even know if we could stand to be around each other without feet of snow keeping us there. But now, here… it's hard to think of a life any less perfect than this.

I mean, yes, he's still a cheeky arsehole who finds pleasure in winding me up. But he makes me laugh every single day. He makes Skye laugh every single day. He loves us both with his whole heart, and what makes it better is that I don't think even *he* knew he was capable of it.

The first time I met him, he was a smooth-talking cocky young man who thought he was a gift to womankind. The second time I met him, he was jaded and moody and thought women should leave him the fuck alone.

Now? Now he's my husband. My partner in business, in life, in parenting. He's my lover, and he's my best friend. He's given me a family when my own are thousands of miles away. And he's given me a reason to laugh every single day.

"Next year we're going to be elves, and you're wearing the hat, too," I whisper as I kiss his neck and run my hands over his wide shoulders.

He flips me over, splitting my legs apart with his knee and pinning my arms down at my sides. "Put it on the agenda next year and we'll discuss the terms of the deal," he says, before returning his mouth to my neck.

My thighs squeeze together around him. He knows exactly how to make me desperate for him and he goes straight to that little spot below my ear every time.

"I'm sick of your deals," I whisper. "I never win them!"

He comes back up and gives me a smirk that turns into a smile. "I think you like it that way. You know what happens to the loser."

I giggle. "What?"

He pushes himself inside me and I sigh like I always do. His arms wrap around me and he rolls us both over, so now I'm the one perched on top of his chest. He grips on to my hips and starts grinding me against him and after a second I don't even remember what we were talking about.

"I fucking love you, Isla," he says, as he leaves me to do the grinding myself and wraps his arms around my body, kissing the top of my head.

"I love you too."

Author Note

Thank you so much for reading and I hope you enjoyed Lewis and Isla's story!

This is a new pen name and a bit of a passion project for me, which all stemmed from moving to this 'fictional' small town in the middle of nowhere in Scotland in my early twenties and missing it like crazy now I live in the city. I thought I'd release a cute little Christmas novella as an introduction to the series I'm launching in the new year which will (hopefully!) be funnier, longer, and cover all aspects of this slightly crazy small town.

Fun fact about this book… I wrote the sex scene while a bunch of my brother's friends were laying new flooring in my house and let me tell you I don't think I've ever been MORE distracted while writing in my life :D I feel like there could have been the makings of a romance novel there… reclusive writer falls for tall, dark handsome workman, throw in the forbidden BBF aspect at the 30% and BAM fireworks. Right? Well, I'm sorry to report they fitted those floors like professionals and only stopped for one cup of tea. They did bring me in a caramel latte when they stopped for lunch though, so all in all, I'm calling it a win.

There's always the boiler…

And I'm rambling. I get nervous writing these things because I love reading them at the end of books but I honestly don't know if that makes me a freak.

If you ARE reading, please consider leaving a review. It would mean the world to me :-)

And if you're STILL reading, I hope you have a wonderful Christmas and a very happy Hogmanay xx

Coming Soon….

If you'd like to be notified please consider signing up to my mailing list: https://www.subscribepage.com/v4y7w1

Gray Sweats Are Ruining My Life

Thick Watches Are Ruining My Life